Siege Town

It had taken the combined efforts of forty men, led by Rick Hartnell, the fastest gun in the west, to hunt down and smash the notorious Lenniger gang, a group of hardened outlaws and rustlers. Now Luke Lenniger was behind bars in the jail at Hammer Bend, awaiting trial and it appeared that the Lenniger gang was finished for good.

But the townsfolk had reckoned wrong. Word reached Hammer Bend that the outlaws were massing in the hills, ready to ride into town and bust their leader out of jail, and then wreak their terrible vengeance on the town itself.

Rick Hartnell had been their saviour once, but could he help again? He was more than forty miles away and time was running out fast. Could he be warned of the impending siege in time? And if so, could this one man rally the townsfolk of Hammer Bend and prevent a savage attack?

Siege Town

Roy F. Copper

A Black Horse Western

ROBERT HALE · LONDON

First hardcover edition 2003
Originally published in paperback as
End of the Trail by Tex Bradley

ISBN 0 7090 7241 4

Robert Hale Limited
Clerkenwell House
Clerkenwell Green
London EC1R 0HT

Typeset by
Derek Doyle & Associates, Liverpool.
Printed and bound in Great Britain by
Antony Rowe Limited, Wiltshire

CHAPTER ONE

Hell Benders

It had taken more than two hours for Rick Hartnell to reach the ford where the river broadened and snaked its way over the dry earth and even then he had to restrain his mount from bolting towards the water and drinking its fill. Finally, stepping down from the saddle, he managed to coax it into merely drinking the measured amount from his hat and then hitched it to the end of a long rope where it was able to graze on the short, green grass which provided the only bit of colour in the whole scene.

Once his mount had been provided for, he took himself down to the water's edge and swilled the alkali dust and grime from his face and neck. The hot sun had scorched his skin more than he had realized and the cool water stung his face, sending little stabbing pains through his cheeks. All the time he washed and filled his canteens, he kept a watchful eye on the trail on the far side of the river, eyes alert for danger. There, the cattle trail wound between the orange-red rocks, lifting over a low rise and vanishing down the far side between a handful of stunted trees and sage. This was new country to him and he had little idea what he might find over that rise. If his luck held, he ought to be close to some town although in this part of the territory they were well scattered and a man had to ride carefully for fifty or sixty miles before he reached a place of habitation. If he were not so fortunate, there could be another hundred miles or so of dead, flat, dreary waste to cross before he came to any place at all.

Throughout that morning, the heat had risen until it was now oven-like, burning and oppressive on his neck and shoulders, lathering his mount as it had picked its way carefully across the Flats from the east, mile after mile in the stifling heat until his horse was covered with dust and sweat and his own clothing stuck to his flesh and his body felt shrivelled and seared.

Refreshed a little by the cool water, he made his way to the shade of one of the trees, settled his back against a rock and rolled himself a smoke, drawing the smoke into his lungs gratefully. He would have felt a little easier in his mind if the message he had received in Canyon City had told him just where he might find the town of Hammer Bend. He had followed the directions given him as closely as possible and judged that he ought to be somewhere within thirty miles or so of the town, but that assumed he had travelled in the right direction all of the time since leaving Canyon City.

For some reason or other, his thoughts went back to that morning when Marshal Simms had asked him to step across to his office. He had guessed then that the other had had something mighty important on his mind. The Marshal's grim face had borne a serious expression and his usually quiet demeanour was taut and hard.

It was then that he had heard, for the first time, of a man who called himself Luke Lenniger, killer and outlaw, a man known to have rustled cattle from several of the big herds to the west of Canyon City. This, the Marshal had decided, was a job for a Ranger who was fast on the gun and could impart some of his own brand of courage to others. The people of Hammer Bend would follow a man who could lead them against Lenniger and his band and Simms had no doubt in his mind that he was such a man.

Now he was on his way to Hammer Bend, to hunt down this band of sidewinders who were holding the territory there in such terror.

He grumbled a little to himself at the way his thoughts were wandering. To find his way to Hammer Bend was his immediate problem and if he had many more miles of these terrible Flats to cover before he got there, he doubted if his mount would finish the journey. Already, anxious to get the job done, he had pushed it to the limit of its endurance. It had carried him well, but back to the east, there had been few water holes and long miles of sunbaked, blistering alkali which he had had to cross and no animal, no matter how good, could be expected to keep on going under those conditions without let-up.

Once he reached the town, he would need only a little while to sound things out and make his decision on what was the best thing to be done. There was always the chance, of course, that Marshal Simms had been wrong in his judgement of the townsfolk in Hammer Bend, and that they could not follow him when he rode against the Lenniger gang. If that happened, he did not intend to plead with them. Men whose heart was not in their jobs would be no use in a posse whose task it was to ride down gunslingers of the Lenniger brand.

He rested out the heat of the day in the shade of the tree which grew on top of a low ledge of rock and gave him ample shade even at high noon. The hot touch of the sun on his face woke him and he knew that he had been asleep for several hours. Already, the blazing disc of the sun had slipped from its zenith, although the heat head still hung over the area and the trees in the near distance shimmered and shook as if he was seeing them through a layer of dark water.

Getting slowly to his feet, he went down to the bank of the river and drunk his fill again, until his belly could hold no more. Now that they were facing the cooler part of the day, it was safe for his mount and himself to drink as much as they could hold. Had it been morning, he would have restrained both the horse and himself, for it was better to ride dry during the heat of noon and early afternoon, than to sweat in the saddle.

Putting his mount into the water, he forded the river, clambered the horse up the far bank, then set off along the wide, broken trail over the brow of the low hill, then dropping steadily downward until he came out of the stunted trees and into more open country, seeing as he had half suspected, that there was more wasteland to cross before he reached the low hills that stood out tantalisingly on the far edge of the Flats. Hammer Bend would be somewhere at the base of those hills, he decided, screwing up his gaze a little against the blinding glare of the flooding sunlight.

As he progressed downward, the heat seemed to increase, reflected off the hot, rocky face of the Flats, dizzying waves of heat and light lancing up at him, burning his eyes and face, the terrible glare forcing its way behind lidded eyes, burning its way into his brain with a fiery agony.

For a short distance, it was still possible to pick out the trail, or some semblance of one where it wound its way over the smooth alkali. Cattle had used this trail at some time in the past, he decided, but many years before and now it was all but obliterated by the drifted dust that had been blown over it by the wind. Now too, there was no sense of direction except for the low hills beckoning him in the distance, and the sun overhead.

He rode for mile after mile in the stifling, sticky heat and always the hills seemed to recede in front of him, moving away as he rode and he realized that it would be nightfall at the earliest before he rode into Hammer Bend. He did not relish having to spend another night under the stars out here on the Flats. In contrast to the burning heat of the day, the nights were icily cold, the heat dissipating rapidly once the darkness came and the sun went down. The stars stood out in the curving arch of the heavens with a diamantine lustre and there were no clouds to help keep some of the warmth in, acting as blankets for the earth below.

The afternoon was almost gone and still the heathead touched its piled-up intensity, with nothing to relieve it. Although he had followed this westward trail for many days now in all of its varying climates and terrain, this day seemed the most punishing to both himself and his mount. Every breath was a labouring of aching chest muscles, a torture of hot, inferno air going down into his lungs, filling his mouth and throat with clogging alkali dust, turning him strangely nervous.

The edge of the saddle was too hot for comfort and the metal pieces of the bridle sent painful flashes of fire into his eyes. Dust clung to the air, worked its way irritatingly into the folds and cracks of his flesh. Pulling up his neck-piece over his nose and mouth, he lowered his head and rode until the country around him finally rose from its flatness into rolling gullies and scree-covered dunes that stretched from right to left across his trail. Clay gulches stood out in shadow as the light of the lowering sun lay across them. Here and there, he saw a lone pine standing out on top of the dunes, an advance sentinel of the hills that lay to the west.

Black and bulky, the hills stood in shadow now as the sun dipped beyond them. Reining his mount at the edge of one of the gullies, he shaded his eyes and stared directly into the streaming sunlight. The town of Hammer Bend was still a way off and he knew with certainty that he would not reach it until well after nightfall. Ahead, the country grew rougher. It had been a terribly punishing ride over the desert but the ground had been flat and smooth; now it rose and fell among rocky outcrops; with here and there, dense timber which would inevitably slow him down.

He rolled himself a smoke, sitting easily in the saddle,

struck a sulphur match and applied the flame to the tip of the cigarette. He had no need of the smoke, it bit hard on his parched palate, but it gave him time to look about him, to take in the shape of the land which lay in front of him.

He was a man who had ridden with danger for so long that it was now a second nature to him to examine every new stretch of country close and keenly before he moved forward. It was just possible that word of his coming had travelled ahead of him. News had a habit of travelling fast here on the frontier and once, some miles back, he had spotted the telegraph poles and wires to the north where they had been laid across a stretch of cleared ground and knew that the chances of someone in Hammer Bend knowing of his coming and the purpose of his mission, were to be rated high.

Smoking, he sat upright in the saddle for a long moment, his right hand lying on the sweat-gummed back of his horse. The smoke had no flavour in his dry mouth and he suddenly felt the urgent need of his dried-out tissues for moisture. Reaching down for his canteen, he held it for a moment, shaking it a little, then withdrew the cork with his teeth and let the warm, brackish water run down his throat.

Ahead of him, nothing moved in the growing dusk. The red sunlight beat against his eyes painfully and his dust-covered lids scraped against his eyeballs every time he blinked. He could just make out the line of the narrow trail now, running in cross-cross fashion among the rocks and into the timber line a mile or so away.

Throwing down the butt of the cigarette, he gigged his mount, urged it on towards the hills. This would be the longest part of the ride for there was a strange feeling in the air about him now, in the world which had begun to turn blue with the setting of the sun and cold with the wind that blew down off the far slopes a feeling of waiting. Like a charge of dynamite with a long, slowly-smouldering fuse attached. Safe and quiet only so long as the fuse burned.

His nerves were jumping a little now and his mind kept reviewing his decision not to stop for a bite to eat, but to ride on, searching it for flaws. He found none, but he hadn't expected to; except that there was a feeling, strong within him, that the trail which lay ahead of him, between there and Hammer Bend, was not quite as empty and deserted as it looked at first glance.

If word had been sent on to town, any killers would have his trail marked by now and they would know all of the dark, safe places for laying an ambush for him. He felt the tension begin to grow, kept his right hand close to the Colt in his holster, his alertness as sharp as the blue-shining, honed edge of the hunting knife in his belt. Tall in the saddle, he rode easy with his left thumb touching the saddle skirt.

The pines lifted tall and straight along the edge of the trail now. He rode slowly, keeping to the middle of the trail as far as possible. Why he felt so certain that they would try to bushwhack him before he reached town, he was not sure. But that tiny spot in the middle of his back, just between the shoulder blades was beginning to ache; a sensation which he had learned from past experience never to ignore. He passed the first clump of trees, rode through their shadow and felt his nervousness increase. It was too dark in there now for him to be able to pick out anyone crouched down in the brush. Every nerve and muscle tense, he kept switching his gaze from side to side, keeping his eyes moving, knowing that it was dangerous, if not fatal, to keep his glance fixed on one spot for any length of time. The tight, empty feeling in the pit of his stomach grew stronger and his chest and face were cold.

A hundred yards along the rocky trail, the sound of the horses' hoofs loud in the stillness, the scrape of a metal shoe on the rock, a sound that carried easily in the growing darkness. Leaning forward in the saddle, he switched his gaze back to his horse, saw its ears suddenly prick the instant he entered an open space between the trees. His head swung sharply to the right. Swiftly, he raked spurs across the animal's flanks. The horse leapt ahead and in that same instant, the two guns flared from the bluepurple shadows among the trees at the edge of the trail.

The horse reared as one of the bullets ploughed a red furrow across its chest. Savagely, Hartnell fought to keep his grip, then urged it forward among the rocks. The Colt was in his right hand as the horse's hoofs came down, the hammer thumbed back. He loosed off a couple of shots at the flashes among the trees, thought he heard a grunt from one of the bushwhackers, but could not be sure as more gunfire broke out from the trees. Now it came from behind him as he whirled the mount into the rocks, slid from the saddle before the horse had come to a halt, and dropped behind a rocky outcrop, worming his way close to the edge of the smooth rock, easing his head up a little and risking a quick look around it. A bullet struck the rock within inches of his head and screamed away into the night in murderous ricochet. He pulled his head down sharply and heard their pounding feet through the brush as they ran forward, hoping to press home their advantage possibly, thinking they had hit him.

Hidden by darkness and the tall rock, he loaded more shells into the chambers of the gun, then pressed himself closer to the rock and waited, eyes fixed on the trees on the far side of the trail. Let them come, he thought fiercely. Let them come as close as they dared. Surprise at finding him still alive, at seeing his fire come from an unexpected direction, ought to force them to break and perhaps run out into the open when he might have a chance of bringing one down without killing him. If he could, he wanted to find out who was behind this attempt to kill him.

From the sound in the brush, he guessed that they had slowed now. Caution had taken over in their minds from their first impetuous desire to close in and finish him. To each, death and danger had become personal things as they came closer to where he lay hidden.

Then he caught a glimpse of the two shadows that edged out into the open on the far side of the trail. Carefully, he eased up the gun, lined it up on the nearer man and squeezed the trigger, felt the heavy Colt buck against his wrist and knew that the slug had gone where he had willed it to go. He saw the man suddenly stagger and sink back as the bullet took him in the thigh, pitching him sideways against his companion.

Hartnell fired again but already the men had fallen back out of sight. He heard one man cursing harshly, the other give a grating moan and then there was the sound of a heavy body being dragged through the underbrush. He stood still, coldly and patiently waiting his chance to put in another shot. When there were no more gun flashes from the brush, he carefully eased his body between two wedging boulders and slid out on to the trail. The Colt in his hand was rock steady.

Another faint movement, this time deeper in the trees. Swiftly, acting on instinct, he fired, then darted across the open trail, threw himself down in the brush, felt the bullet fan his cheek as gun flame tulipped in the darkness. Crawling to one side, he backed away from the edge of the trail, let his weight down slow and easy, balanced on his feet like a prizefighter, ready to move in any direction in a split second.

Sucking in a long, heavy gust of air, he let it go through his nostrils in slow, short pinches, standing rigid now, unmoving, staring off into the dimness. The two men were silent now and it was a case of seeing who could outwait the other. It was not a long wait. Patience and a cold wash of anger had made rock out of Hartnell so that he could have waited for ever without moving.

He knew that it was waiting that would break the nerve of the other men. Bushwhackers were not usually men with nerves of steel otherwise they would meet their opponents in the open, in fair fight, instead of skulking in the shadows, shooting a man in the back without any warning.

He heard a long, drawn-out groan come from the wounded man. It was a sudden need for air and movement which had betrayed the other and the men seemed to know it for within seconds they began to fire with a pure recklessness, raking the bushes to his left where they clearly guessed him to be, wasted ammunition because he was more than ten feet away and none of the flaying bullets came near him.

Jerking up the Colt, he fired three shots into the trees, heard the men moving deeper into the timber, crashing through the brush. There must have been a narrow trail a little distance away, hidden by the trees for a moment later, there was the sudden thunder of hoofbeats, of horses being pushed hard through the trees. Thrusting his way forward, ignoring the sharp, whiplike branches that raked his unprotected face and shoulders, he reached the trail, saw the two horses as they rounded a sharp bend twenty yards away, knew that he would not get in another shot before they were gone out of sight, had time only to glimpse the man on the back of the second animal, lying low in the saddle, evidently badly hurt. Then he thrust the Colt back into leather and rubbed his chin thoughtfully.

Listening, he heard the steady abrasion of the horses retreat and fade into the distance, until the sound was no more than a faint echo, soon gone altogether. He walked slowly to his own mount, pausing for a moment to examine the ground at the edge of the trail, then stepped into the saddle, rode out along the trail as it wound and twisted into the rocks, his mind filled with angry and bitter thoughts. There had been blood on the brush beside the trail back there and he knew that one of the men was bleeding profusely, that he would have to get back into town before he started making inquiries. The two men had too much of a start, knew this country far better than he did, for him to hope to catch up with them before they reached town.

The town of Hammer Bend lay in a large elbow in the tall hills with the pine covered crests towering up to the west and curving around on two sides. He made a slow swing in the saddle as he rode into the main street – a double row of buildings with long, low overhanging roofs which jutted out over the boardwalks and left them in shadow, even in the blazing heat of high noon.

He rode between the single-storied houses on the edge of town then into the centre where another trail, cutting down from the direction of the hills, linked with the main street. Here were the bank, saloons, hotel and Sheriff's Office, all within sight of each other. The livery stable, he noticed, lay just beyond the hotel.

He gigged his mount forward. As he dismounted, a man drifted out of the rear darkness and came forward to peer closely at him.

'Reckon you'd better give your mount a drink first,' he said. 'Looks as though you've ridden a longways. The trough's over yonder.' He jerked a thumb towards the street trough, stood back with his shoulders against the wall of the stable and lazily rolled himself a smoke, drawing the match slowly down the rough wall. By the light of the quick flare, Hartnell saw that in spite of his apparent disinterest, the man's eyes were fixed on him, watching him intently, assessing every move he made. Giving his horse a quick drink at the trough, he led him back, took off his gear, hung it on one of the pegs on the wall by the stall, then led the sorrell inside.

All of this time, even though he did not look up, he knew that the other man was watching him, had made no move, even though his face was still in shadow. Hartnell moved past him, brushing close, then stepped out into the street once more, turned and went over to the hotel, signed the register, and climbed the stairs to his room on the top floor, overlooking the street.

The water in the tall pitcher burned the skin of his freshly scorched face but it removed the hard mask of white alkali dust which had formed during the long ride; and the cool water slaked his thirst as he up-ended the pitcher and let what remained in it drain down his throat, filling his belly until it could hold no more.

After he had put on a fresh shirt from his bag he made his way down the creaking stairs into the long dining-room. There was still that strange feeling of restlessness bubbling up inside him as he sat down, waiting for his meal.

He was halfway through it, eating ravenously, when Lee Henshaw's voice reached him from just at the back and a second later, the man had crushed down into the other seat at the table.

'Didn't expect yuh so soon, Rick.' he said quietly, his gaze travelling swiftly to every corner of the room. 'Heard yuh were on your way but that desert trail can be a bad one. Never thought yuh'd make such good time across it.'

Rick nodded, chewed reflectively for a moment on a mouthful of beans, gestured towards the food with his knife, but the other shook his head.

'Thanks, but I've already eaten, Rick.' he said. 'I've been keeping my eyes open for the past week. This is one hell of an uneasy town.'

'I guessed that as soon as I rode in. I got a special welcome all to myself.'

Henshaw lifted eyebrows that seemed to have been bleached almost white by long exposure to the sun.

Rick went on. 'A couple of jaspers tried to bushwhack me back there along the trail. I winged one of 'em but they had horses holed up in the trees and they got away.'

'Yuh got a look at either of 'em?'

'Nope.' Rick shook his head slowly, drained the hot coffee from the cup. 'It was too dark to see anything. But I do know that I hit one of 'em in the leg and he was losing a hell of a lot of blood when his companion got him away over the back of his horse. He'll need to be seeing a doc pretty quick to get that wound patched up.'

Henshaw gave him a close, studying glance and for a moment some question seemed to be balanced in his mind. Then he shrugged his shoulders slightly.

'I can keep my eyes open for anything like that, I reckon. But they won't try to get help openly and there are one or two sawbones in town who'll do something like that with no questions asked and nothing said.'

'And Lenniger? What about him?' There was a tightness in Rick's voice as he sat back in his chair, pushing the empty plate away. He pulled out his tobacco pouch, rolled himself a smoke and then handed it to the other.

'Ain't picked up any smell of him yet,' grunted Henshaw.

'I'm betting he's around here someplace. Probably up in the hills yonder, jest bidin' his time. He'll come when he's good and ready.'

'Yuh figurin' on waiting here for him?' Surprise edged the other man's voice. His eyes narrowed just a shade. 'You reckon that would be wise? He's got plenty of men with him up there in the hills.'

'I know that. This town has a reputation for shelterin' the wild ones. That's why I'm here.'

'You won't find it easy to get any men to follow you if you decide to ride against Luke Lenniger.' There was conviction now in the other's voice. He leaned forward in his chair. 'Don't reckon Sheriff Haggarty likes the idea of going after Lenniger.'

Rick gave a quick, tight grin. 'I can't say I blame him. From what I've heard of this *hombre*, he's a cold-blooded killer and not the sort of man to get into a corner. He's got quite a reputation as a gunslinger and the men with him will shoot first and talk afterwards.'

'Then whatever you do, move easy in town,' said Henshaw warningly. 'All strangers riding in here are watched.'

'You don't have to tell me that. I've already met up with a couple of 'em back on the trail who took more than a passing interest in me. You got any idea who could have told 'em I was on my way and the trail I'd take? Seems to me they knew exactly where and when to lie in wait for me.'

'Could have been Frank Brand in the telegraph office. He's the only one likely to get the message except for myself and the Sheriff.'

'Would he talk to them?'

Henshaw pressed his lips together in a tight line. 'He would with a gun in his back.' he murmured grimly. 'That goes for most of the folk in the town.'

'Just what I figured.' Rick drew deeply on the smoke, relaxing. His stomach growled contentedly at the food and the energy of the supper he had just eaten was a stimulant, washing away most of the tiredness of the long journey. Sitting back, he fully enjoyed the laziness and the feeling of luxury that came on the heels of so long and punishing a ride. 'But there should be such a thing as the law.'

'Not here there isn't. At least, not as far as Lenniger is concerned. The hills out there are too full of places where men can hide. How do yuh expect a posse to cover that, even if you could get 'em to ride with yuh?'

'There'll be somebody in town who knows where they're hidin' out, if we can only get 'em to talk,' said Rick, soft and final. He stubbed out the butt of his cigarette, got to his feet, stood for a moment looking down at the other. Then he said softly. 'Stick around, Lee. Make sure that nobody suspects why you're here until we're ready. I'll have a parley with the Sheriff tomorrow.'

Sheriff Haggerty was a short, thick-set, surly-looking man but he greeted Rick with an unexpected heartiness of manner, waved him towards the chair set in front of the wooden desk. The early morning sunlight shone in dimly through the dust-covered windows that looked out on to the street.

'I'm sure glad that you got here so soon, Mr Hartnell,' Haggerty said. His eyes were narrowed a little, giving an oddly mean cast to his bluff features. 'Yuh didn't have any trouble on the way?'

'Matter of fact, I did,' Rick said quietly. 'Two *hombres* tried to shoot me down along the trail. I'd like to find out who they were if I can. Do you know any sawbones in town who might be helping these critters?'

The thick brows lifted a fraction. 'Don't reckon so,' Haggerty said, swinging around in his chair and staring out of the dusty window into the street. He seemed to have a strange habit of moving his gaze around whenever he was talking so that he didn't appear to be listening too intently to what was being said to him. 'But it would be only human for any doctor to treat a wounded man if there was a gun on him. You figgerin' on talking to some of the folk in town?'

'That had crossed my mind,' Rick admitted. 'I just want to find out who those men were, see if that might give me a lead on the Lenniger gang. Once I find out where they have their hide-out, then I'll need your help, and that of a posse, to ride out and finish 'em off.'

'Understand now, Mr Hartnell,' Haggerty went on quickly. 'When I wired for help, I didn't figger on involving too many of the folk of this town. They said they'd send me a man who was quick with a gun, but I didn't mean to—'

'You never thought that you might become involved in this fight too?' said Rick harshly. There was a note of disgust in his hard voice. 'Trouble is that if you want to make this town a decent place to live in, make it possible for a man to go about his business without having the threat of being shot hanging over his head, then you've got to have law and order and you've got to enforce it. You've got your tail in a crack and you've shouted for help.

Well, I'm here and I'll lead you and your men out there into the hills and bust this Lenniger gang wide open. But I don't aim to fight these men alone. I need your help in this job, just as badly as you seem to need mine. I hope that we understand each other.' He stared at the sheriff inflexibly.

The other tried to meet his gaze, but within seconds his eyes shifted to another part of the office and he looked unhappy. Then he laughed nervously. 'Do you know how many gunslingers Lenninger has with him in the hills, men ready to ride with him and shoot this town to pieces?'

'I can guess,' Rick said drily. He heaved himself lithely to his feet and walked over to the window, stood for a long moment in silence, his back to the sheriff. 'Only if you do as I say, they're not going to do it!'

'How in tarnation do you plan to stop 'em?'

'By hitting 'em before they get the chance to ride into town. There must be somebody in Hammer Bend who knows where they're hiding out. Somebody who's scared to talk. We've got to find him and get the information out of him. You don't want your town shot up. Some of you have to help.'

'All right, Hartnell. All right. I've got no choice. I asked for you to come here, I suppose.' His face seemed to have lost its colour, until it was almost grey. 'And if you don't find out where they are?'

'Don't worry. I will.' For a moment, Rick hesitated, then moved towards the door, turned to face the other. 'Let's go and have a talk with the local sawbones. How many are there in town?'

Haggerty rose to his feet, reached for his hat and clamped it on top of his head. For a moment, he stared emptily at nothing, then moved towards the man waiting at the door. 'Three,' he said throatily. 'Shouldn't take us too long to question 'em.'

Doc Thornton's office was a hundred yards along the dusty street. Sheriff Haggerty paused in front of the door with the ancient painted sign that swung over it, then knocked twice before going inside, with Rick close on his heels. The furniture in the room was old, but well-kept and Rick ran an appreciative eye around him. Certainly Thornton seemed to have established himself well with the citizens of Hammer Bend and had obviously been there for some time.

'Anybody home?' called Haggerty loudly.

There was a brief pause, then the door at the far end of the room opened and a small, wizened man stepped through, peering up at them through thick-lensed spectacles.

'Who is it – oh, it's you, Sheriff. Something wrong?'

'We ain't sure yet, Doc,' grunted the other. 'You had anyone visit you in the last day or so with a gunshot wound in his leg?'

Rick watched the other closely, trying to figure out for himself the effect of Haggerty's words, but the little man did not seem to have been put out by the question and there was nothing on his face or in his eyes to suggest that he had a guilty conscience.

Thornton shook his head slowly, almost wonderingly. 'A gunshot wound, you say? Nope, ain't had anybody with a wound like that. Why'd you ask, Sheriff?'

'Seems that Mr Hartnell here was shot at on the trail into Hammer Bend yesterday. Claims he hit one of the *hombres* in the leg and they headed in the direction of town. We figured that they would have to come to a doctor to get the wound fixed and we're checking on it.'

Thornton shook his head again. 'Afraid I can't help you there, Sheriff. You asked anybody else?'

'We're just on our way.' Haggerty moved back towards the door. He threw Rick a swift, enigmatic glance. Outside, on the boardwalk, he asked: 'You figure he was tellin' the truth back there?'

Rick nodded. 'He seemed to be. Let's ask more questions.'

Ten minutes later, after questioning the second man, they were in the small outer parlour of one of the houses almost on the edge of town. Rick had eyed it closely as they had walked up to it. Certainly, if anyone was coming to get a bullet taken from his leg, they would choose someplace close to the outskirts of town so as not to arouse too much suspicion, even after dark. This looked to be a likely place.

His train of thought was broken as the doctor came in. Tall and thin-faced, he eyed Rick closely before swinging his gaze back to the Sheriff. Rick noticed the prominent adam's-apple which bobbed up and down nervously in the man's scrawny throat and the way his eyes kept shifting from the Sheriff to himself and then back again, uneasily. A doctor shouldn't be so nervous, he thought to himself.

'Sorry to barge in on you like this, doc,' said Haggerty, 'but there was a shooting out on the trail yesterday and we know that one of the gunmen was hit in the leg. We were wondering if he'd come here to get the wound fixed and if—'

'I'm afraid you're wasting your time if that's why you've come here, Sheriff,' said the other, seating himself in one of the tall, high-backed chairs. 'Am I the kind of man who would treat an outlaw, a killer?'

The other had the precise way of talking of an educated man but he seemed to talk a little too quickly to make it sound natural. There was no doubt in Rick's mind that this man had something to hide.

'If you have a gun laid on you, then you do as you're told,' Rick broke in thinly.

The watery gaze swung back to him for a moment. Then the other said: 'Just where do you fit into this, Mister?'

For a second, Rick felt the harsh anger rise strongly in him as he faced the man but when he spoke, his tone was even enough. 'I happen to be the man they tried to kill. And I'm quite certain that they were members of the Lenniger gang.'

He instantly saw the spark of fear that sprang unbidden into the other's eyes.

'Did they come here?' asked Haggerty. He took a pace forward until he stood directly in front of the other, staring down at him.

The doctor swallowed thickly, his gaze flicking to the window of the room and then the door as though expecting retribution to fall on him within an instant if he should divulge the truth, then he nodded his head rapidly. He seemed completely unnerved.

'I had to do it! It was just like you said. One man stood over by the wall and held his gun on me while I operated. The bullet was in his upper leg. It had been bleeding a lot, but they insisted on riding back out of town as soon as I'd finished and they threatened they'd ride back into town and kill me if I breathed a word of it.'

He stirred uneasily in the chair, shifting his feet. Sheriff Haggerty said: 'So they were part of the Lenniger gang.' He fixed his gaze on Rick. 'Just like you suspected. Now we're getting someplace.' He spun on the man in the chair. 'What time was this, Jethroe – and where did they go when they left you?'

'I-I don't know, Sheriff. That's the truth. It was after dark, I'm sure of that because I'd closed the surgery. In fact, I was getting ready to go to bed when this knock came at the door. I reckon it must have been nearly an hour later when they left. They must have ridden along the mountain trail, I think.'

Rick nodded. It made sense and it all fitted in with what he had thought. Even with the threat of Luke Lenniger hanging over the town, Hammer Bend would have been just a little too hot for those two outlaws and they had ridden straight up into the hills to their hideout to give this latest bit of information to the gang leader himself. He wondered what Lenniger would do now that he knew that he was still alive and kicking. Make another attempt on his life? He turned the possibility over in his mind.

Certainly they would have to get rid of him before he became too much of a menace to them and managed to get a posse together to hunt them down in the hills. Once he managed to swing the townsfolk over on to his side, once he succeeded in raising them from their fear and apathy, they might ride out with him and that would mean big trouble for Luke Lenniger.

He breathed deeply as the Sheriff turned away from the man still seated in the high-backed chair. There were still a great many things they did not know. He did not doubt that the doctor who had patched up the wounded man knew nothing of the hideout of these outlaws. That was something they had to find out before they could move against them.

CHAPTER TWO

Killer in the Dark

It was just on sundown and there were seven thin-faced men sprawled around the rough timber cabin set high in the foothills of the mountains to the west of the town of Hammer Bend. Coming in on them at a slow, easy walk, Virgil Kahler felt a touch of acid dryness in the back of his throat. Beside him, hanging low and helplessly in the saddle, Pedro Carotta, lay slumped forward with one leg stiffly thrust out of the stirrup, his face grey and drawn. The bandage around the flesh wound in his leg had become sodden with blood where the jolting ride had opened the wound afresh. They had passed the two rifle-toting guards further back among the rocks overlooking the trail and he had noticed the hard glances they had given him, knew that this was nothing to what they could expect from Lenniger once the other learned they had failed in their mission, that Hartnell was still alive and in Hammer Bend.

Maybe they were riding straight into a deadfall. Like as not, this could be the last ride for both of them. Lenniger had indicated only too well that he wanted Hartnell dead before he had a chance to reach Hammer Bend and his tone had left no doubt in either man's mind as to the reward of failure.

He felt a little wave of blind, futile anger build up inside him. It had all been the Mex's fault. If only he had waited until they had had Hartnell dead in their sights before there was a chance for the other to dive for the cover of the rocks, they could have nailed him for sure.

Arriving outside the tall, timbered cabin, he reined in, dropped from the saddle and eased the cinch a little before turning to face the group of waiting men. Two of them came forward at his signal and helped Pedro from the saddle.

A moment later, the door of the cabin was thrust open and Lenniger came out; a big, raw-boned man clad entirely in black leather, his features like a hunk of roughly-hewn granite, eyes a very pale blue, unwavering like those of a rattler getting ready to strike.

The other's gaze flickered momentarily to Pedro, then swung back sharply: 'What happened to him, Virgil?'

'He got it in the leg, boss. I took him to Doc Warner in town, got it fixed up as best I could before bringing him out here. Reckon the ride wasn't too good for him. It's been bleedin' again.'

'I can see that.' The other inspected Virgil for some seconds in dead silence, his eyes glinting sharply in the pale light. 'And you figger that this sawbones can be trusted to keep his mouth shut in case anybody starts asking awkward questions?' he rasped.

Kahler nodded quickly. 'He won't talk. I made sure of that. He was so danged scared he had a job getting the slug out, his hands were shaking so much. Reckon he knows for sure what'll happen to him if he does get careless.'

'And Hartnell. Is he dead, like I said?'

'Well . . . he—'

'Quit mumblin',' roared the gang-leader. 'Either he's dead – or he ain't!'

Kahler shrugged, then jerked a thumb towards Pedro as the injured Mexican was helped towards the hut. 'He gave us away, the damned fool. I asked you to let me go alone, that I could do that job best on my own, but you reckoned the Mex was a good man with a gun. He fired on Hartnell before we were ready, gave him the chance to get under cover. I reckon he paid for his foolishness.'

'So he's still alive and in Hammer Bend right now?' Something ominous had come over the other's face and entered his voice. The look on his rough features boded ill for the other. 'Now we've got to change all our plans. Pretty soon, he's going to swear in half the town as a posse and they'll come up here into the hills trailin' us.'

'They won't dare to ride against us.' Kahler tried to force conviction into his tone. 'We know every trail and fork in these here hills. We could empty em' out of their saddles before they knew we were lying in wait for 'em.'

'You think so.' Lenniger glanced tightly at him. 'Seems to me you ain't never heard of this *hombre* Hartnell. They say he's the fastest man alive with a gun. More'n twenty men killed in fair fight down along the border. Why'd you reckon that Haggerty would go to all of the trouble to call in a gunshooter like him, if he wasn't satisfied that he was the best man for the job, maybe the only man who could get the townsfolk to follow him up here into the hills?'

'I still reckon that he'll find it difficult to get anybody to ride with him except mebbe for Haggerty and one or two deputies,' suggested one of the other men, backing up Kahler. 'Can't be many *hombres* in town willin' to risk their lives ridin' up into the hills lookin' fer trouble.'

'To hell there won't.' Lenniger swung on the man sharply, his face flushed with sudden anger. 'I tell you I know this *hombre*, 1 know his rep as a gunman. There'll be plenty in town who've heard of him too. You go on thinking you're safe here and you'll wind up dead. Hartnell isn't a man to be foolin' with.'

He moved in the direction of the cabin. 'Reckon we'd better talk this thing over and pronto, plan the best way to get rid of Hartnell before he makes any more trouble for us.'

Impatient anger still edged his tone as he went inside. Pedro had been laid out on the low bunk against the back wall of the cabin. Occasionally, he twisted himself around, groaning as the movement shocked pain back into his body. Lenniger gave him a sharp glance, then looked away.

'I figure we may be safe for a few days,' he grunted harshly as he lowered himself into one of the chairs. He rolled and lighted a smoke for himself. 'Nobody in town knows of this place and—'

'Ain't you fergettin' Old Man Thompson, boss?' broke in Kahler. 'Reckon he's one *hombre* in town who knows too much about this cabin here. If Hartnell should get around to talkin' to him . . .' He deliberately left the rest of his sentence unsaid, but he knew from the sudden look on the other's face that Lenniger had realized the danger there.

Slowly, the gang-leader nodded his head. 'You're right, I had forgotten him,' he said harshly. 'Seems we can't leave him in town to spill everythin' he knows to Hartnell and the sheriff. We've got to make sure he doesn't talk.'

His glance travelled slowly around the table. 'Rozer!' he murmured finally. 'Reckon you'd better make sure of that. You know where to find him?'

'Sure, boss.' The lean-faced gunman nodded, the lids drooping lazily over his narrowed eyes. His grin was an evil thing. Flicking a glance in Kahler's direction, he said softly: 'I figure that this time, somethin' will be done right around here.'

'All right.' Lenniger nodded tersely. 'Get going.'

Pushing back his chair, the gunman rose to his feet, checked his rifle for a moment, then strode out of the cabin. Moments later, there was the sound of hoofbeats moving quickly into the distance along the trail.

*

Sometime during the night, a flurry of sound outside the hotel window reached down into the depths of Hartnell's brain, down into the part of him that never slept. It was like the fall of a dry board in an empty house, followed by the single, rattling echo. He heard it as he would a sound in a dream, but it succeeded in waking him from his sleep and he sat up in the iron bed, shaking his head a little and staring about him into the darkness of his room. For several moments, he sat absolutely still, ears straining to pick out any repetition of the sound that had woken him, but he heard nothing. His mouth was dry and his surroundings strange so that when he finally swung his feet to the floor, he had backtracked with his memory and by the time he reached the window, drawing aside the flimsy curtains and peering out into the deserted street outside, he was able to allow his gaze to travel swiftly along the silent rows of houses and buildings on both sides of the street, alert and watchful for any movement there. There was one solitary yellow light shining in one of the windows far down the street and after a moment's reflective pause, he guessed that it was in the window of Doc Warner's office near the edge of town. He eyed it musingly for several seconds wondering why the other should be awake at that early hour of the morning, then a sudden movement at the edge of his vision attracted his attention and he swung his head back sharply.

He noticed that there was a horse tethered to the hitching rail outside one of the saloons on the far side of the street perhaps fifty yards from the hotel. It was standing patiently, and only the flick of its hind leg had brought its presence there to his notice.

The nagging feeling that something was wrong, terribly wrong, was strong within him and the sight of that lone animal standing there merely served to heighten his suspicions. Swiftly, he pulled on his shirt and trousers, then buckled the gunbelt around his middle, slipped on his boots and made his way silently out of the room, down the creaking stairs as quietly as possible and out through the entrance, slipping the iron bolts back. A swirl of cold night air thrust at him and he shivered a little as he stepped through into the street, glancing quickly in both directions.

He crossed the street, paused on the other side, his right hand within an inch of the butt of the Colt in its holster, ready for trouble. He could see no one in the shadows, but the thought of that sound he had heard a few minutes earlier was still with him and the more he thought about it, the more convinced he was that it had been a gunshot. He slid around the side of the saloon, stood there in the shadows. He was debating. If someone had ridden into town, ready to kill, then the killer was still there, had possibly spotted him the moment he had come out of the hotel and crossed the street, might still have him in sight, was only waiting for him to step out into the open once more before sending a bullet into the shadows.

There was no way of knowing where he was. He tried to recall anyone who lived in the small buildings in this area along the street from the saloon, but he could remember none of them, certainly could figure out no reason why any of them should be marked for a slug.

It was not in him to wait. He knew within moments that he would have to hunt. He had travelled too far and hunted killers too long to stand in the shadows and wait for the man to come to him. At that moment, he wasn't quite certain why he was so sure there was a killer loose in the streets of town, but it was a feeling he chose not to ignore. Hugging the walls of the buildings here as closely as possible so as not to expose himself to anyone watching from any of the windows or doorway, he crossed a gap between two of the houses in three long, swift, easy strides, gained the shadowed wall of the next building without drawing a shot, breathed a little more easily as he crouched down, flicking his gaze from one side to the other, every nerve and sense strained for the slightest hint of danger from any direction.

The next houses all sat very close together. Some looked as if they had not been lived in for many years, but there were others which were clearly still occupied, with curtains drawn over the windows. At each end of the houses he paused and looked along the dark shadows to the narrow street which ran at the back of them where the thick layer of white dust threw up a faint glow which could be readily picked out from the darker background.

Then, close at hand, someone stirred. There was the faint clink of metal against brick, as if spurs had touched the wall of one of the buildings and been dragged along it as their owner had slithered away, deeper into the shadows. He pulled himself up into immobility and listened intently, trying to figure out where the other stood. Perhaps if he stood quite still and waited, he could break the other's nerve, force him to make a move and give himself away.

The seconds ticked by with an agonising slowness. Whoever it was who stood in the shadows, he made no move to edge further now that he guessed Rick was close enough at hand to pick out any movement. Rick let a couple of minutes slide by and then backed away silently along the front of the house, back to where the narrow alley led back to the rear of the buildings. He paused for a moment, then moved quickly along it, into the rubbish-filled alley at the back and along the shadows there until he came up behind the man in the shadows. Cautiously, he threw a glance around the corner of the building. Now that he was looking out towards the main street of town, it was possible to see the other quite clearly, standing with his body pressed tightly against the wall in a half crouch, the gun held rigid in his right hand. As he had expected, the other's back was towards him and he paused only for a moment before stepping into the alley, the Colt in his right hand lining up on the other's back.

'Just hold it right there, mister,' he said tightly. 'And drop that gun.'

He saw the other stiffen abruptly, then hesitate. For a second, he thought that the gunman intended to make his play there and then, to risk a quick shot at him. The thought certainly seemed to live for a moment in his mind for his body was held taut and as rigid as the weapon in his fist. Then he suddenly realized the futility and stupidity of making such a move. His shoulders relaxed fractionally, he opened his fingers and let the gun drop with a clatter on to the stones of the alley.

'That's better,' Rick murmured as he went forward a couple of paces, still keeping his eyes on the other. 'Seems you've got a little explainin' to do to the sheriff.'

'You ain't got nothin' on me,' said the other harshly. 'Just who are you, anyway, creeping up on a man like that?'

'Reckon it ain't your place to start asking the questions.' Rick's voice was deliberately hard. 'I find you skulking about in the alleys with a drawn gun. Seems to me you meant to kill somebody, or you've already done it.' He thought he detected a tightening of the other's body at that remark, but in the darkness, he couldn't be sure. The other had moved over to the wall, his hands still held away from his sides. Instinct warned Rick that although he had dropped his Colt, the other man was still dangerous.

'Better move out into the street where I can take a good look at you,' he grated. 'Move and don't try any funny—'

Too late, he saw that the other had been shamming all the time, that his left hand, hidden from Rick's sight by his body had picked one of the loose bricks from the wall, his fist closing tightly around it. Even as Rick brought up the barrel of the Colt, lining it on the other's body, finger tightening instinctively on the trigger, the outlaw had swung around, twisting his body from the hips, and the brick caught him high on the temple, hurling him back against the far wall, half-stunned, lights flashing vividly in front of his eyes and pain exploding savagely in his skull.

Somehow, as he fell, he managed to retain his grip on the Colt. Pain jarred redly through his head as he struggled to keep a hold on his buckling consciousness, to get to his feet. Dimly, he was aware that the other had made no attempt to go for the gun on the ground, but had run for the mouth of the alley and out into the main street, his feet pounding on the rough stones.

Somehow, Rick got to his feet, stood swaying for a moment as the blood rushed pounding to his head, throbbing viciously behind his eyes. With an effort he moved drunkenly forward, reached the end of the alley and stared off into the street. Vaguely, he managed to make out the man as he scrambled into the saddle of the waiting horse, pulling swiftly on the reins, jerking the animal's head around and urging him along the street in the direction of the hills.

Sucking air down into his lungs, he fought to steady himself, to stop his vision from blurring. There was no point in trying to follow the gunman. He had too much of a head start now, would soon lose himself in the hills.

Slowly, he moved out on to the broadwalk, striving to walk upright, steadying himself against the wall with one hand. A moment later, he realized that he still held the Colt in his right hand. With a quick movement, he thrust it back into its holster.

Ahead, a little light filtered through from the direction of the Sheriff's Office and a second later, the door was thrust open roughly and Haggerty stepped out into the street, buckling on his gunbelt, blinking a little as he stared about him. He stopped when he saw Rick, then came forward a little more quickly.

'Jest heard some *hombre* ridin' out of town like all the little devils were after him,' he muttered thinly. 'Thought I heard a shot too, a while back.'

'That's what must've wakened me. I spotted the horse tethered over here and came across for a looksee. This gunhawk was holed up in one of the alleys waiting to take a shot at me, I guess. When I crept up and took him from behind he lobbed a brick at me, knocked me cold for a minute, then made off.' He threw a rapid glance along the street. 'Reckon he got clean away this time, whoever he was.'

'You didn't happen to get a look at his face?'

Rick shook his head. 'Nope. Afraid not, Sheriff. Too dark in there and he kept his face turned away from me.'

'Reckon he would at that,' grunted Haggerty musingly. 'No sense in gettin' a posse together and ridin' after him now though. He'll be somewheres in the hills by now.' He lifted his head sharply. 'But I reckon you'd better get the Doc to take a look at that bump on your head.'

'It's nothin'. Just a scratch.' Rick glanced back along the deserted street. If anybody else had heard the ruckus, they were remaining inside, out of harm's way. Probably this was a common occurrence and nobody bothered when it happened, going on the assumption that it was no business of theirs and a man could get himself killed poking his nose into something that didn't concern him. 'I guess the polecat must've been shootin' at somebody back there. Think we ought to take a look-see?'

Sheriff Haggerty fell into step beside him, their boots clumping hollowly on the wooden boardwalk. The smell of the abandoned houses came to them with the other night scents, damp and musty, with dust getting into their nostrils and the back of their throats. The first house they entered, beside the alley where the gunslick had been hiding, was empty.

A thick wooden beam lay behind the door and dust lay thick on the floor of the lower room once they had pushed their way inside, staring about them in in the chill dimness. A rat scurried from one corner of the room, up on to the tilted beam, paused for a moment to glare at them out of red, baleful eyes, before leaping down and rushing for the dark shadows once more. Here, this was the only sound that disturbed the stillness. Haggerty struck a match, peered about him in the pale, flickering yellow light which did not even penetrate into the dark, shadowed corners.

When he spoke, his voice sounded oddly strained and loud in the clinging silence.

'Nobody been in here for years. Even the dust on the stairway yonder hasn't been touched. Nothing here.'

They moved back to the door. Rick could smell the dust that had been dragged up into the air by their own feet, a dust that had settled there over the years and been dried into a fine powder, clinging to everything. They crossed the dark mouth of the alley. The house on the other side had neat print curtains drawn over the windows, had that lived-in look which told of the touch of a woman's hand.

'Who lives here?' asked Rick, nodding towards the building.

'Old Matt Thompson and his daughter Julie.' Haggerty's brows were drawn suddenly tighter together over his deep-set eyes and he set his feet quickly on the boardwalk, rapping loudly on the door. 'He's one of the old-timers here, used to do a lot of prospecting up there in the mountains, about ten years back. Made a lucky strike and then came down into town to live. The hills were no place for a girl like Julie.'

'Can you think of any reason why anybody should want to shoot him down?' asked Rick.

'Nope.' The other shook his head. 'But ain't you jumpin' to conclusions? We don't know that either of 'em have been shot and—' He paused. There had been no answer to his knock, but a moment later, Rick distinctly heard the faint moan that came from somewhere inside the house. Haggerty had clearly heard it too for he twisted the handle of the door, stepped back when he found that it was locked and motioned to Rick.

'Somethin's wrong all right.' Together, they put their shoulders to the door. Wood and hinges creaked under the strain. Then, with a sudden snap, the lock gave and the door swung inward. There was an old lamp set on the low table, and although it had almost burned out, it still gave enough light for them to see by.

Rick followed closely on Haggerty's heels, saw the girl lying on the floor near the door at the far side of the room. The Sheriff went down on one knee beside her, turning her over a little.

'She's only unconscious,' he said through clenched teeth. 'Whoever it was, they must have knocked her out.' Carefully, he lifted the girl in his arms and carried her to the long couch, laid her on it, then straightened up with a grunt. 'I'll see what I can do for her,' he said quietly, 'you'd better take a look around.'

Nodding, Rick pushed open the other door and stepped through into the room at the rear of the house. A cold blast of air touched his cheek as he went in and a swift glance told him that the window at the far side of the room had been smashed. Still treading carefully, he went over to it, examined it closely, saw what he had begun to suspect. There was a neat round hole in the middle of the splintered glass where a bullet had passed through the pane.

Backing slowly away from the window, he stumbled over the body on the floor a moment later. Pausing, he struck a match and found himself staring down into the face of the old man who lay there, face upturned towards the ceiling. For a second, Rick felt sure that the other was dead. There was an ugly red stain on the front of his shirt and his chest was so still that he did not seem to be breathing. Then, bending close to the other, he made out the faint, rasping breath that wheezed in and out of the other's lungs.

'Haggerty,' he called loudly.

The other appeared in the doorway, stood peering into the darkened room for a second. 'What is it?'

'I think it's Thompson. He's been shot. Somebody plugged him through the window yonder, got him in the chest.'

'Hell.' The other let the word go savagely, stepped forward and bent beside the old man. Gently, he felt for the pulse, then nodded half to himself.

'He's pretty badly hurt. That slug must be close to his heart. It'll be a miracle if he lives. I'll get the Doc.' Scrambling to his feet, he hurried off. Crouching down beside the old man, Rick heard the Sheriff's footsteps on the boardwalk outside as he made his way quickly along the street. Why should that killer want to shoot down an old man like this? he wondered inwardly. With most of the buildings here empty and deserted, there seemed little likelihood of him having been shot by mistake. The killer had known exactly where to come, had crept up to the rear of the house and shot carefully and calmly through the window.

Was this anything to do with Lenniger, he mused. At the moment, he could see no connection, apart from the fact that if any man in town knew the hidden trails of the hills it would be Matt Thompson. But surely the outlaws had nothing to fear from an old man such as this. He represented no danger as far as they were concerned.

His train of thought was broken as the Sheriff came back into the room. He stared across at the other. 'Is he still alive?'

'Only just breathing,' Rick said grimly.

'The Doc will be here in a couple of minutes. I've told him to come along pronto.' He faced Rick over the inert body on the floor. 'Why would anyone want to kill Matt?' His tone was harsh and edged with tension and anger, barely kept under control.

'I've been trying to figure that out for myself.' Rick pushed himself slowly to his feet, went over to the holed window and looked out into the backyard now lying in shadow. 'You reckon that Lenniger can be at the back of this?'

'Lenniger?' Haggerty glanced up in surprise. 'Can't think how. Don't seem to be any sense to this shootin' to me.'

'There's got to be some reason for it,' persisted Rick. 'Men don't go sneaking around town, shooting down old men without warning, unless they have a reason.'

At that moment, the doctor appeared at the entrance of the room. He carried the lamp which he had brought with him from the front parlour. Setting it on the table, he motioned towards the Sheriff. 'Could you fill up the lamp for me, Sheriff,' he asked. 'I think there's some oil in the corner yonder. I'll need some light in the room if I'm to make an examination. I don't want to move him until I know how badly he's been hurt.'

Haggerty brought over the can of oil and filled the lamp carefully, turning up the wick as far as it would go so that the warm yellow light flooded into every corner of the room. The doctor went down beside Thompson and gently eased the sodden shirt from the wound. Finally, he looked up. 'That slug will have to come out if he's to have any chance at all. Fortunately, he's got the constitution of an ox and that's going to stand him in good stead during the next few hours. I'll want you both to help me.'

'What about Miss Julie?' asked Haggerty.

'She'll be all right in a little while. At the moment I'm more concerned about her father.' He looked up at the Sheriff shrewdly. 'You got any idea who did this?'

The other shook his head unhappily. 'Hartnell here heard the shot and came over to check. There was a gunman in the alley outside, but he managed to get away, had a horse waiting for him.'

'I see.' The other gave a quick nod. 'Lift him carefully on to the table here. Try not to move him any more than you can help. The slightest jerk might kill him while that slug's still there.'

Half an hour later it was finished. The doctor wiped his hands on the rough towel, then went into the parlour and Rick heard him talking in a low voice to someone, guessed that the girl had recovered consciousness.

He went through into the other room. The girl was

sitting up on the low couch with the doctor's arm around her shoulder, supporting her. She still looked dazed, but some of the look of memory was creeping back into her eyes and face.

Putting a hand up to her head she gingerly felt the lump on the back of her skull, winced as pain jarred through her head.

Haggerty's voice came harshly from the open doorway. 'Do you recall anythin' of what happened, Miss Julie?' he asked officiously.

'Don't you think this is scarcely the time and place to start asking these questions, Slim?' grunted the Doctor. 'She's had a bad crack on the head and you can't expect her to be able to talk to you without some rest. By the morning, I reckon she may be in a fit condition to talk.'

Haggerty's face was flint hard. 'I figure that the morning might be too late, Doc,' he said tightly, coming further into the room until he stood over the girl. 'Your father's been shot bad, Miss Julie and I think you either know who did it or why it was done. Either way, it's going to be a big help to us.'

The doctor answered for her before she could speak. 'I don't see where this questioning is leading, Sheriff.' His tone was a little pompous. 'What harm can a few hours' wait do? Whoever it was has got clean away by now. You couldn't catch him if you set off with a posse right this minute.'

'Mebbe so. But if I figure it right, Luke Lenniger ordered Matt to be shot. And I want to know why before it's too late and he comes ridin' into Hammer Bend with that outlaw band of his, ready to shoot up the town.'

A look of apprehension crossed the old doctor's face at that remark and he turned his head and looked quizzically down at the girl. Rick watched her closely. She had furrowed her brows in thought, shaking her head a little. Then she said hesitantly: 'All I can remember is that I heard somebody moving about outside the house, but when I went to the door and called out, nobody answered. As it was late, I thought that perhaps I'd been mistaken, or it had been a drunk from one of the saloons. But when it came again, I went out to take a look. Pa was sleeping in the back room, and I didn't want to disturb him so I didn't make no sound. Then I heard this gunshot from the back of the house, heard Pa cry out and came back inside. I thought I heard somebody behind me as I got inside, but then everything went black and I don't remember anything else.'

Her eyes widened a little as realization of what she had said came to her and she tried to get to her feet, to move shakily towards the rear room, but Haggerty reached out a restraining arm and drew her back.

'He's asleep now, Julie,' he said quietly. 'There's nothin' you can do. The Doc reckons that he'll be all right if we let him rest and don't try to excite him. That's why I've got to ask you questions.'

She slumped back on the couch, her eyes a little fearful, but he could see that she was doing her best to pull herself together.

'I figure that Luke Lenniger sent one of his hired killers into town to gun down your father. I think maybe you know why they should want him dead.'

'I can't think why . . .' she began.

Rick said softly: 'Your father used to be a prospector up yonder in the hills, didn't he?'

'Why yes, but—'

'And he'd know all of the old Indian trails, all the places where a gang of men could hide out with little fear of being found. He'd know for instance, where Lenniger might be hiding out, and perhaps the best way to get there without being spotted by any of his look-outs.'

He knew by the sudden, almost startled look on her face, that what he had suspected had been very close to the truth.

'You think that's why they wanted to kill him? Because

they felt that he might talk to you, tell you where to find them?'

'I'm sure of it,' said Rick earnestly.

'Oh, God.' For a moment she buried her face in her hands. 'Why can't people leave us alone? All we wanted was to come and live in town without trouble from anyone and now this has to happen. Why, why?'

Slowly, Rick said: 'It's because the ways of violence never seem to change, I'm afraid. These men don't want the country here to grow up, to have its own laws and become civilised, because they see a threat in that to themselves. They know that once law and order comes to the frontier, they'll be hunted down like the criminals they are and brought to justice. So they'll fight every inch of the way, fight tooth and nail to stop any progress.'

For a moment, the girl's gaze fell on to the guns he wore low at his waist and then up to the ugly bruise on his forehead and her lips tightened just a little. 'Where do you fit into this?' she asked pointedly. 'You look like a man of violence yourself.' There was, he recognized, a tinge almost of regret and dislike in her voice but he thought little of it at that moment.

'You can only meet violence with violence,' he said quietly. 'There's no other way. When you've been in this business as long as I have, you'll know that to be true. These outlaws respect no laws which aren't backed up by force, for that's the only argument they can understand. It won't be until they're all caught and brought to justice, or killed, that men like the Sheriff and myself will be able to shuck off these guns.'

'And in the meantime, innocent people are going to be shot without warning.'

'This was something nobody could have foreseen,' broke in the Sheriff. 'But if you know anything at all, you can help us round up this bunch of killers and make this territory a safer place in which to live.'

'Do you think you'll ever manage to do that?' she

inquired archly. She was on her feet now, swaying a little, but with a determined expression on her face as she pulled herself together. She watched Rick steadily now, her gaze not moving from his face. Then she said: 'I'll tell you all I know, but there isn't anything. If my father knows anything that could help you track down these ruthless killers, then he never divulged it to me, or anyone else.'

Rick sighed, swung his gaze to the old doctor. 'How long before he can talk, Doc?' he asked tersely. 'You can guess how important this is, not just to us but to everyone in town.'

The other rubbed his chin with his fingers. Rick knew that it was unseemly to be discussing something like this in front of the girl, but it had to be done. He wished there might be some other way, but there wasn't.

'Not before morning, if he recovers consciousness. I can't guarantee anything though. He's been badly hurt, you saw that for yourselves. I've done all that I can for him at the moment. Rest and freedom from excitement are essential now.'

'I reckon he'll help us if he can,' affirmed Haggerty stolidly. He glanced at Rick out of the corner of his eyes. 'I think we'd best go back and catch up on our broken sleep and leave this until the morning. I'm damned sure that varmint won't try anythin' again. He'll be miles away by now, racing back to Lenniger with the news that Matt is dead.'

Rick nodded wearily. Out in the street, the cool night air revived him a little. The bruise on his forehead was throbbing painfully now, but he chose to ignore it. Back in his room at the hotel, he paused for a long moment in front of the window overlooking the street. There was still a pale yellow glow filtering from the Thompson house and as he watched, the door opened and the doctor came out, stood for a moment silhouetted against the light as he spoke with the girl, then he stepped out on to the board-walk and made his way slowly along the street. Three minutes later, the light went out in the window of the house across the street.

Rick stretched himself out on the low bed, his hands clasped behind his neck as he stared up at the ceiling over his head. He doubted if he would be able to sleep much more that night even though there was a deep-seated weariness in his limbs, and a dull ache suffused behind his eyes. Things were happening here a little more quickly than he had anticipated. Evidently by now, Lenniger had heard that he had slipped through the net which had been thrown around the town to prevent him from getting into Hammer Bend alive and Lenniger was doing all he could to tie up the loose ends before questions were asked around town and somebody decided to talk.

The thought of what was to come rolled powerfully through his mind. If the old man regained consciousness the next morning and could tell them what they wanted to know, it would suit their plans to get a posse of men together right away and ride out into the hills, get this thing over with before Lenniger could make ready to meet them. If the outlaws decided to ride down into town and have the gunfight there, it could mean a lot of innocent men and women becoming involved, possibly killed. He would much prefer to take the fight to Lenniger, even though at first sight it might appear as though the ground then would be one of Lenniger's choosing and not his own.

A lot was going to depend on whether Haggerty could raise a posse quickly. There were bound to be men in town who knew how to handle a gun. Whether they would be willing to go up against a man like Lenniger was a different matter.

Looking across at the girl, Rick felt the misery that was holding her, saw it written on her face. On the bed, in the small room, into which the sunlight was just beginning to filter, the old man lay white and unmoving. Under the tan of his face where it had been burned brown by long exposure to the wind and sun, the skin seemed bloodless. On the other side of the bed, the doctor straightened up, looked across at them.

'He seems to have come through the worst of it. His constitution has stood him in good stead. I reckon he ought to be able to answer your questions, but you can't talk to him for long. Ten minutes. That's all I can give you. Then you'll have to leave him to me.'

Haggerty moved forward until he stood beside the doctor, staring down at the wounded man in front of him. Almost gently, he asked: 'Matt – can you hear me?'

The man on the bed stirred, tried to lift his head to look down at the broad band of cloth around his chest, then let his head sink back on to the pillows once more as if the effort had robbed him of his feeble reserves of strength. Then he twisted his lips and tried to grin away the hurt of his injury.

'That you, Haggerty?'

'Yep, it's me, Matt. Who did this? You got any idea?'

'Never saw him, Sheriff. Too dark back there. He just shot through the window, I reckon.'

'We figure that it was one of Luke Lenniger's men, that he sent him into town to kill you because you know a little too much,' broke in Rick suddenly.

The pain-filled eyes turned towards him, studied him closely from beneath lowered lids. Then the bloodless lips moved again and the husky whisper said:

'Who're you, mister?' Questingly, the man's gaze swept back to the Sheriff.

'He's all right, Matt. I asked him to come here to help us finish Lenniger and his gang for good. You can talk freely in front of him.'

'Reckon the only reason they'd want to kill me is that I know where they may be hidin' out up there in the mountain. The old Saunders place, up on the eastern column.

From there, they can watch the whole of the valley, watch anybody riding up for miles.'

Rick turned to Haggerty. 'You know this place, Sheriff?' he asked tersely.

The other gave a quick nod. A look of understanding had crept into his eyes. Musingly, he said: 'That could well be it, Rick. But it doesn't help us any. If they can spot us comin', they'd be ready for us and once behind those rocks with a handful of high-powered rifles, they could empty us from our saddles without any trouble. A handful of men could hold off an army at that point.'

'Which explains why Lenniger chose it as his hide-out. But isn't there any other trail we could take which would let us take 'em by surprise?'

Haggerty pondered that for a moment, then shook his head slowly. 'Never heard of any and I reckon I know these parts as well an anybody.'

The man on the bed turned his head and a low, cackling laugh escaped from his lips. 'Then I reckon you don't know enough, Sheriff,' he whispered. For a moment, a spasm of coughing prevented him from speaking, but he waved his hand impatiently as the doctor moved forward to make him lie still. 'Stay where you are, Doc,' he rasped as the soggy coughing eased. 'I know what I'm doing.' With an effort, he succeeded in pushing himself up on to his elbows. 'There is a trail which will bring you out on a wide ledge right behind those varmints. And they'd never know you was there until you hit 'em with gunfire. But you'd have to set out early and ride well around the mountain to the west, then cut up into the hills where a stream comes down out of the rocks. Used to be an old Indian trail there, but we found it when we was prospecting on that side of the mountain. Gets pretty rough on the way up and it'd take you the best part of the night to reach the top.'

'But the trail is still there?' persisted Rick tightly. He felt a growing sense of excitement deep within him. There seemed to be a chance left open for them after all. He guessed that this was some information which even Lenniger knew nothing about, otherwise he might have made doubly certain that Thompson did not live to talk.

'Should be. Can't tell you what it'll be like now. This was more'n fifteen years ago. Never been used since then, I reckon. You'll find an old cabin about halfway up built against the side of a rock face, sheltered from the winds. After you get there, you'll have to travel for another two, mebbe three, miles before you reach the ledge. The trail winds and turns there and in places there's only a slide of hard-packed earth.'

'Reckon we ought to be able to find that, even in the dark,' grunted the Sheriff. He moved away from the bed, turned towards the door. 'I'll get some men together, Rick, and we'll ride out within the hour. Reckon the best time to take these critters will be just around dawn when they're least expectin' it and we've got a bit of light to see by.'

The old man sank back exhausted on the bed, worn out by his long speech. But there was a look of contentment on his face now which had not been there earlier.

CHAPTER THREE

Gunsmoke in the Hills

Night began to reach in from the east as the group of riders came up to the narrow stream that bubbled swiftly down the side of the high foothills. Led by Rick Hartnell and Sheriff Haggerty, they had ridden out of Hammer Bend earlier that day, before the sun had risen to its zenith and had taken the rough, winding trail to the west of the town for several miles before swinging north again, around the great rocky curve of the mountain where it thrust deep into the valley that lay to the south. There, they had turned up into the hilly country, leaving the smooth flatness of the plains behind.

Rick dismounted and let his horse drink from the clear, rushing water. Around him, the other men were doing the same, grim-faced men who now rode with the thought of vengeance in their minds. The narrow trail on the far side of the stream was just visible where it climbed steeply into the thickening brush. They still had a long and arduous ride ahead of them and their mounts were already tired by the long, dusty ride from town, a journey through the heat of the day and the coming cold of the night. There seemed no point in pushing their horses too far and too hard.

The hills were silent now. There did not seem to be a single living thing abroad apart from themselves and the quietness had a strangely disturbing effect on the men. They seemed to draw together, to talk in low, muted whispers as though each man was afraid of being overheard. It was a signal of things to come which the shadowed, timbered hills, by their very silence, seemed to heed. He thought of Luke Lenniger as he moved a little away from the others, along a deep trench that had been cut along the bank of the dark-rushing stream. The thought of the other evoked a rush of that cold, bleak anger that seemed to have been riding him for a long while now. Although not a lawman, in the sense that he wore no silver star, no badge on his shirt, this deeply-instilled hatred of men like Lenniger and those who rode with him, the wild bunch of the hills whose law was the sixgun, stemmed from an episode in his life many years before, when a band of men such as these had swooped without warning on the small, innocent township and left a trail of death and destruction in their wake. The fact that most of these men had been renegade Mexicans from south of the border, anxious to kill as many of the hated gringos as they could, had made too deep an impression, too lasting a scar on his mind for him ever to be able to forget.

Haggerty's voice reached him from the growing darkness a moment later and he turned to find that the Sheriff had left the others and was standing close behind him.

'You seem unsure of yourself a little,' said Haggerty softly. 'Somethin' on your mind? You reckon we may be ridin' into a deadfall?'

Rick shook his head slowly at that. 'Just thoughts that keep running through my mind,' he muttered shortly. 'They're of no consequence, believe me.'

Haggerty said nothing for a long moment, staring out into the dark bulk of the timbered slopes that hung over them almost on the point, so it seemed, of overbalancing and streaming down to crush them like a vast wave of bleakness, frozen just on the point of breaking. He rubbed his chin hard with the back of his hand, flesh rasping against the growth of beard there. His head turned a little and he looked anxiously at the shadowed bank on the opposite side of the stream.

'Hell, but I hope that Matt was right all the way along the line when he told us about this trail.' More anxiously now, he went on: 'You don't think that at times he might have been talking out of his head. A gunshot wound like that can do funny things to a man, make him forget important details.'

'That's a risk we've got to take, isn't it?' Rick grunted. 'We've come this far, we can't turn back now.' He cast a swift glance at the men by the bank of the stream, the milling group of horses, men in the saddle riding up and down somewhat aimlessly. 'Though I doubt if it would take much to get them to turn back. I reckon that the further we go, the less they like the idea.'

'They're scared, sure enough,' nodded the other heavily. 'I know that. But I figure they'll stay with us and see it through. Mebbe you don't know it, but most of 'em are here only because of you and your reputation as a gunman. I'd never have got them to ride with me alone.'

Rick shrugged. 'Maybe if you'd got the men together and ridden against Lenniger before he got too big you could have finished him then without too much trouble. This is what happens whenever the ordinary citizens of any town refuse to look things squarely in the eye and fight for what they know to be right. When those outlaws move in and try to take over – that's the time to go against them. If you give them time to consolidate their position, to start intimidating people, you're finished. They can only grow and flourish on fear.'

'All very well to talk like that,' said the other defensively, 'but it ain't no easy matter being Sheriff of a town like Hammer Bend, trying to swear in deputies. You've got to take what you can get. Too many of 'em are scared to lose their lives if they go up against a man like Lenniger. Can't really blame 'em, I reckon. Not many of 'em are professional gun-toters and to ask 'em to step up against killers like these and on their own territory, is a bit much.'

'Sure.' Rick shrugged his shoulders, loosening the muscles of his body. Already, now that the sun had gone down, there was a rush of cold air coming down the side of the hill, stirring the top branches of the nearby trees. He could imagine how jumpy the other men were. Knowing the reputation of the owlhoots who lived in these hills, it was easy to imagine a man behind every tree and rock, fingers curled around the triggers of high-powered rifles, ready to drop them from their saddles without any warning.

They made their way back to the waiting men, treading carefully through the coarse grass that grew in wild profusion along the strip of marshy ground bordering the stream. Swinging up into the saddle, he sat easy, watching the rest of the men.

'All right. Let's go, boys!' said Haggerty sharply. He put his mount into the stream, the water foaming and churning around the beast's legs. Rick followed, felt the bubbling, frothing water hit the animal against the chest as the current born high in the hills, caught it. For a split second, the horse stumbled on the smooth rock of the stream bed, then regained its feet and moved surefooted across the stream which at this point was little more than twenty feet in width. Around them was a silence so still that a man had only to lean out in the saddle to be able to touch it. A clinging, tangible silence that was built, rather than broken, by the splash of the horses as they piled across the stream.

Lifting his head, Rick saw that although the sky was clear overhead and to the west, with the stars beginning to show, a dark curtain had built up into the eastern heavens, was sweeping in from the horizon, crowding out the bright stars. Thunder rumbled low and menacing in front of them. No dry riding for them this night, he thought wryly, not with lightning forking the dark eastern heavens. But it would help them when they finally approached the hide-out of the outlaws, would shield and drown the sound of their mounts thrusting through the brush and would make the gunhawks themselves a trifle lax and careless in their vigilance. A wet and tired man was less likely to keep a sharp look out than a dry, alert one.

There was still a trail of sorts here, stretching into darkness ahead of them. It snaked and bent through first growth pine, would lose itself occasionally in thick brush which had grown in from both sides. Rick noticed this and felt a little easier in his mind. It showed that old man Thompson had been right in one respect.

This trail had been forgotten for years, had not been used at all since those early days of the men who had come up here to dig the ore from the hills and pan the grains of yellow gold from the swift-running streams, who had lived with privation and fear. The chances seemed high now that Lenniger and his bunch knew nothing of its existence even though, according to Thompson, it would bring them out on to the wide ridge overlooking the cabin which was the hideout of the outlaws.

The riders grew weary in their saddles. Thorny strands raked and whipped their faces and shoulders as they rode. Twisting trunks of tall trees rose and lifted in a wild confusion on all sides, hemming in the trail. Even here where there was shelter of a kind, the wind held a bitter edge. Cold closed around them like a blanket and Rick fought the chill in his body with a conscious effort as he forced his mount forward with quick rakes of his spurs.

The ground rose quickly now, steep and treacherous, rocky and slippery. The horses stumbled forward, wearied by the gruelling ride, seeming to sense in some strange animal way that worse lay ahead of them, that the journey was not over by a long way. More lightning spilled and forked across the beserk heavens. Still no rain though, as the thunder roared and rolled above them, crashing on all sides. Sudden gusts of wind snatched at the branches of the trees. Rick's heels drilled against the flanks of his mount, keeping it moving. It was not often that weather like this could spook horses, they were too used to it, but it had been known to happen.

Again and again, the wicked whiplash streaks of lightning flared vividly over the rearing crest of the mountain, followed within seconds by roaring thunder that rumbled along the rough slopes echoing away across the plains below.

'Keep those horses moving!' Haggerty, head bent low, yelled the warning. The next second the trail wound out into open ground and a solid wall of rain hit them viciously, drenching them to the skin within moments. It was impossible to sit upright in the saddle in the face of that terrible onslaught. Eyes narrowed, head pulled low, Rick allowed his mount to pick its own way forward.

No need for silence now as they rode on through the storm-wracked night. The thunder would drown out any sound they could possibly make. A sudden vicious flare and a lightning bolt struck earth. A crash and a tree fell, burning furiously; a lone pine that stood out on a rocky limb of ground.

This was old for the riders, this scene of incredible beauty and violence; old and yet still frightening. Out of the corner of his eye, Rick saw them fight to control their mounts as they bucked and plunged. Still some miles to go before they reached their destination.

There was a primitive, raw savagery in the scene about them as they rode on through the storm. Wind and rain beat against their faces, thunder roared at their eardrums, and every few minutes the vivid glare of lightning dazzled them. Straining his eyes, Rick pushed his sight through the darkness that lay ahead looking for landmarks. The old man had said that they would pass one of the old cabins halfway along the trail. As yet he could see no sign of it. All around them, now that the trees had thinned, were the wild craggy ledges that stretched around the side of the mountain. Here and there, the trail was no more than a slide of hard-packed dirt, barely three feet wide and already the lashing rain was beginning to wash it away. In places, it had become virtually impassable.

Instinctively, the men formed up into single file, keeping close to the wall of rock that rose sheer on their left. Occasionally, a man cursed loudly as an out-thrusting rock tore at his knee cutting the skin; but even that was better than risking the sheer drop of perhaps two hundred feet on the other side of the trail.

They crossed another narrow creek, the water spuming whitely over the rocks. Beyond it, they moved into trees again. The trail widened here and Haggerty gigged his mount, came up abreast of Rick.

Leaning sideways in the saddle, he called: 'See anything yet of that hut the old man mentioned?'

Rick shook his head, dashed the stream of raindrops from his eyes as the water ran through his plastered hair, down his forehead, and spilling from the wide brim of his hat. 'I figure that we should have sighted it by now,' he yelled back, raising his voice to be heard above the dull roll of thunder.

Over their heads, the storm seemed to be passing over, going on towards the other side of the mountain. He couldn't be sure, but he thought the sky was clearing a little, low down in the east as the storm passed over as quickly as it had come. Through the water and thirty yards inside the timber, they hit the trail again as it snaked and looped up the side of the mountain. They climbed now in a series of switchback courses, the cold wind chilling them to the bone, their sodden clothing chafing and irritating as it slapped painfully about their bodies in the night wind.

Here among the trees, there were open patches of

earth and rock with some vegetation clinging precariously to them and the trail was no more than five feet wide. But there was no precipice on one side now and they made better time, urging their horses forward. The flagging mounts were both tired and doubtful of this long-unused trail but they responded gallantly at each touch of the rowels.

Then, almost before they knew it, the trail widened abruptly, the trees fell away on either side and there was a bare rock face rising up on their right and almost directly ahead, just visible in the darkness and slanting rain, a darker shadow which slowly materialised out of the night; a ramshackle log cabin set against the sheer rock face, sheltered from wind and rain. Gratefully, they urged their weary mounts forward, reining in in front of it.

'So he was telling the truth, after all,' said Haggerty. He swung down from the saddle, glanced up at the sky where the cloud was still thick although beginning to break here and there. 'Reckon we can rest here awhile and give our horses a chance to blow.'

The rest of the men dismounted, threw reins over their mounts' necks, stretched cramped limbs gratefully. A few tried to roll cigarettes, turning their backs on the wind and rain, dragged the smoke into their lungs. The air was still bitingly cold, but here they were sheltered from the full fury of the storm.

'You figuring on ridin' on through the night, Sheriff?' growled one of the men harshly. He rubbed the back of his hand over his face where the thorn branches had cut deep, bloody furrows in the flesh.

Haggerty forced a quick nod. 'We've got to get behind those varmints by dawn and we still have a long way to go. I know how you men feel, I'm just as cold and tired as you are. But we've got no choice.'

'Everybody's tired,' protested the other harshly. 'So's the horses. No supper and likely no breakfast when we get there.'

Haggerty drew himself up to his full height. 'We're in a goddamned hurry.' His voice had an edge to it now. 'Ten minutes and then we move on. By dawn, with luck, we ought to have 'em.'

The man turned away, grumbling, obviously dissatisfied, but he made no effort to communicate his feelings to the other men. A few had gone for shelter inside the long wooden cabin, but over the long years the roof had fallen in and there were piles of debris scattered on the floor, blocking their way.

Sheriff Haggerty stood at the side of the cabin, staring off into the night. The storm was now moving away towards the west, the thunder rumbling in dull, fading echoes, the lightning now low on the horizon. Wiping the rain from his face, he muttered thickly. 'We might get a dry ride from now on. I'd feel easier if 1 knew what those owlhoots were doing right now.'

'You think they may be riding down into Hammer Bend, expectin' to find us there?'

'Could be. That thought had crossed my mind, I must admit. That's why I'm so anxious to be moving on. I know how tired these men and the horses are, but until we get there and take those outlaws, I won't rest easy in my mind.'

The riders checked their mounts on the low rise of ground that stood out amid the creeks and gullies on the mountainside. The dull, grey wash of an early dawn showed far in the east and around them, details were beginning to emerge from the darkness. With the main group of men among the thick brush twenty yards back along the trail, Rick rode ahead slowly with Haggerty, their mounts picking their way carefully and soundlessly through the rocks.

Haggerty reined his mount a few moments later and pointed in silence. Coming up to him, Rick reined his mount, peered into the grey dawn. Some fifteen feet away, the ground dropped sharply at the edge of the ridge and a moment later, there came the clean sound of a shout echoing up from below. Slipping from the saddle, they edged their way forward, hands hovering close to the butts of the guns they carried at their waists.

Close to the edge, a clump of coarse bushes jutted out over the ledge and Rick crouched down behind them, parting the thorny branches as he peered down into the long, wide clearing that lay stretched out below them. Looking down, he discovered the two men who stood close to the wooden cabin in the centre of the clearing. Beyond them, the trees jutted up to their fullest height, hiding the cabin from the trail that lay down the side of the mountain. It was an excellent defensive position. He could well see how these outlaws were so confident that they could not be attacked without warning. But in spite of this, they would have posted outlooks along that other trail up from the south-east. With luck, they would not be expecting an attack from this direction. As far as they were concerned, it was impossible to scale the mountain from this direction.

'Seems they're still here,' he whispered to the Sheriff. 'Better get back there and bring up the rest of the men.'

'They may try to make a break for it along the trail yonder,' pointed out the other. 'Reckon we ought to send a couple of men in that direction to head 'em off in case they try it.'

Rick threw a quick glance along the trail, then nodded. 'Good idea.' He cast a quick glance at the sky. 'It'll be light soon. We've got to hit 'em now before they have a chance.'

Haggerty motioned to the men standing back from the ledge. A moment later, they had moved forward, taking up their position, hard-faced men who held their Colts and rifles in tight fingers, sighted them on the two men and the cabin below.

'They've got two men scouting out yonder along the trail,' said Rick in a hushed tone.

'That's what I figured,' said Haggerty.

'What else did you figure?'

'That if we can rake that cabin down there from one end to the other with Winchester fire, the slugs ought to go clear through that flimsy roof and catch those outlaws in there without any chance to escape unless they get out into the open.'

'You could be right,' agreed Rick. He cast an appreciative glance at the cabin. The roof looked as if it would afford little protection against rifle fire. A quick glance and he saw that the men were in position. Haggerty lifted his left hand, a look to right and left, then he dropped it swiftly. One after another, the rifles barked, sending a rain of fire down into the clearing below. The two men outside the cabin were hit instantly, their bodies jack-knifing forward as the slugs tore into them. One man spun on his heel, his right hand diving instinctively for his gun, but it never reached it. The weapon was still in its holster when he died.

It was grim and dispassionate business. There could be no quarter for these killers. Every man down there in that cabin deserved to die and the men who had ridden out from Hammer Bend knew this and went about their work with a cold ruthlessness.

The firing swung across the cabin. All of the men among the rocks knew exactly what to do. It seemed impossible that anyone could remain alive in that wooden building down there, but shots were coming from the windows and the bullet-splintered doorway.

Rick narrowed his eyes, peered down. A bullet struck the rock within inches of his body and whined into the distance in murderous ricochet. Jerking his head savagely to one side, he fired instinctively at the rifle flash which had showed clearly from the window beside the door. The crash of gunfire echoed and re-echoed around the rocky canyon, pouring into the cabin below. Quite distinctly, even above the whine of bullets, he heard one of the men below die, the harsh shriek of pain as the slug tore through clothing and flesh, through bone and muscle.

'They're tryin' to get away on the other side!' One of the men yelled the warning.

Rick swung round, eyes narrowed. He still lay flat, but by lifting his head a cautious inch, he noticed the group of men make a quick dash from the cabin, bodies bent almost double as they darted across the stretch of open, rocky ground towards the trees less than thirty feet away. Two men died before they reached cover, their bodies pitching forward a couple of yards, dead on their feet, their onrushing momentum carrying them forward before they dropped.

The hammer of Rick's gun clicked against a spent cartridge. Cursing savagely, he plucked fresh slugs from his belt, thrust them into the empty chambers. Dimly, he heard Haggerty's voice, lifted above the sound of gunfire.

'Back to the horses. Follow them! Ride them down. . . !'

The men scrambled to their feet, boots slipping on the wet rocks as they ran for the waiting mounts. Sorrel studs racked down the side of the ledge, out on to the clearing, out towards the trees. Guns barked as the riders from Hammer Bend cut down the racing outlaws.

On the ledge, Rick Hartnell got slowly and cautiously to his feet, finger resting on the hammer of the Colt. He made no attempt to move back towards his mount, tethered ten yards away. He had seen what the others had not. That Luke Lenniger had not broken clear of the bullet-riddled cabin. Either the outlaw leader was dead, wounded, or had decided to play things his own way, reckoning on everyone riding after his men when they broke cover, giving him the opportunity to slip away, ride back up into the hills. He must have realized by now that he had been taken by surprise, that there was little chance of defeating this posse which had ridden out to take him. Lenniger no doubt prided himself on his scout system. Now he must have known that he had been betrayed, that either one of his men had talked, or old man Thompson had not been killed before he had told all he knew.

Rocks caught and tore at his hands and knees as he slithered snake-like down the ledge, feet striking the solid ground at the bottom with a jar that went through him, spreading into every limb. Sucking a gulp of air down into his lungs, he gritted his teeth, then edged towards the rear of the wooden cabin, the Colt rock steady in his right hand, eyes alert for any movement. Close to the wall of the cabin, holding himself hard in against the side of the building, he tried to guess the other's actions, assuming that Lenniger was still alive, still in there, waiting.

Slowly, he crept up the side of the wall until he reached the open doorway where it had been cut and splintered by the terrible volume of fire that had been poured into the building. Chips of wood lay in every direction and here and there he noticed the neat round holes where the slugs had penetrated the thin wood. Pausing, he pressed his ear to the side and listened intently, holding his breath until it hurt in his lungs. Around him, the sky was brightening. Soon, the sun would be up, turning the dawn into full daylight.

He slid a couple of inches nearer the edge of the door, body pressed tight into the wood. He stood there for a long moment, debating: 'If Lenniger were still in there, waiting his chance to move out into the open and then escape into the rocks, he could be just inside the doorway, listening as intently as he was for the sound of pursuit to die away into the distance, and to make sure that there was no one else around.'

There was no way of knowing exactly what the other would do, and Rick was in no mood for waiting. He had come too far to meet up with this man. All of the cold hatred suddenly boiled up inside him, threatening to spill over the tight control he held over himself. Setting one foot forward, he balanced his weight carefully on it, then thrust himself forward, the gun jerking up in his hand as he flung himself sharply to one side, going down on one knee. He fought to get his eyes accustomed to the gloom inside the cabin in the few seconds he had.

Lenniger's gun exploded a few feet away and Rick felt the slug fan his cheek as he went down. The other was a dark shadow, crouched against the far wall of the cabin, beside one of the low, metal bunks. Swiftly, he pulled up his gun, before the other could fire again. His finger tightened on the trigger, the Colt jumped in his hand and he knew, the moment that he fired, that the bullet had gone where he wanted it to.

The burned powder bloomed crimson in the dimness and the room roared with the quick explosion. By the glare, he saw Lenniger reach up to his full height, then slump back against the wall, the Colt falling from his nerveless fingers, his other hand going up to the red stain that showed on his shirt.

He groaned and twisted his body against the wall. Rick went forward, plucked the other Colt from its leather holster, then pushed Lenniger roughly into the middle of the room.

'You hit me in the shoulder,' said Lenniger, grinding the words through his teeth. 'That wasn't a wise thing to do.'

'Mebbe not. Mebbe I ought to have killed you,' said Rick thinly. 'But I figure that the folk of Hammer Bend might want you alive. They'll have a rope ready for you after you've been tried. It's up to them now.'

Lenniger's lips twisted into a sneering grin as he fought down the pain in his smashed shoulder. 'You don't reckon they can hold me in that jail in Hammer Bend, do you?' he grunted.

'If you're banking on your men to bust you out of there, forget it.' Rick swung back as footsteps sounded outside the cabin. 'They're well scattered now, if they haven't been killed. No use botherin' with them any more.'

'That's what you think,' snarled the other harshly. He

still held on to his injured shoulder.

Haggerty came into the cabin, his gun drawn. He relaxed when he saw Rick, then moved across to Lenniger. 'So we've finally run you to ground, Lenniger,' he gritted. 'Reckon your band is finished too. they've high-tailed it out of the territory and I doubt if they'll stop until they hit the border. And with you in jail, I figure we've seen the last of you.'

'Don't be too damned sure of that, lawman,' muttered the other sullenly.

The rest of the men came back into the clearing, riding slowly, as Rick and the Sheriff followed Lenniger out of the cabin. One man swung down easily from the saddle, walked towards them.

'We killed five of them,' he said, with a trace of pride in his tone. 'The others headed south, into the Badlands.'

Haggerty gave a quick nod. 'They won't stop until they're out of the territory,' he affirmed. 'Without Lenniger to lead 'em, they're finished.' He glanced round at Rick. 'This is a good day's work. Once we get this pole-cat back to town, I'll get word through to the circuit judge and we'll try him as soon as he gets here.'

They found Lenniger's mount hidden among the trees towards the rear of the cabin. Setting him in the saddle, they rode back in a tight bunch to town, cutting down out of the hills, into the rough foothills and then out on to the wide plain. The sun lifted clear of the horizon, a blazing disc that sent waves of heat into their faces, dizzying and sickening.

By the time they reached Hammer Bend, the men were leaning forward, weary, in their saddles, their faces a mask of brown where the dust had worked its way into the folds of flesh. They rode in a tight bunch down the main street, the sound of their horses' hoofs beating a dull tattoo on the dusty street. The people on the boardwalks watched in silence, their eyes fixed on the outlaw leader who rode a little way ahead of them, staring straight ahead, not once looking to right or left.

Past the tall bank building they rode, reining in front of the Sheriff's office and jail. Haggerty slid from the saddle, moved forward, stared up at the outlaw implacably.

'All right, Lenniger. Get down and move inside. Don't try anythin' or I'll blast you and save the judge a job.'

Lenniger twisted his lips into a thin sneer. He said coldly, 'You'll regret this, Haggerty.'

'Sure.' The Sheriff gave him a savage push as he dropped to the ground. 'But you won't be around to see it. Why don't you take a look at things as they really are, Lenniger? You're finished. Your little run is over and there's only the rope waiting for you.' He grinned viciously. 'Without those owlhoots who ran with you in the hills, you're no longer the big man you thought you were.'

He thrust the other towards the door of the office, followed him inside. Most of the men were now dispersing, riding their mounts towards the saloon. Rick watched as they pushed open the batwing doors, then vanished inside, before following Haggerty into the office.

'Reckon they'll live it up for a while,' he said to Haggerty.

'Guess they deserve it,' he muttered. He went behind his desk, took out the large bunch of keys. 'Go ahead of me, Lenniger.' He held his Colt ready, still expecting the other to make trouble.

There were four small cells at the rear of the building, standing off a central passage. Opening one of the doors, Haggerty thrust the outlaw inside, then locked the door behind him. Stepping back, he grunted. 'I'll get the doc to have a look at that shoulder of yours. Not that you deserve it. I ought to leave you in there to bleed to death, but I figure the townsfolk would rather see you dangling from the end of a rope.'

Lenniger glared at him, then stalked to the rear of the cell and sat down on the low metal bunk, staring straight ahead of him. He gave no further indication that he was aware of their presence there.

Haggerty spun quickly on his heel, walked back into the office, placed the cell keys in the drawer of his desk, snapped it shut, then thrust the Colt back into its holster. Slowly, he lowered himself into the swivel chair, placed his feet on the desk and rolled himself a smoke.

Reaching into one of the other drawers, he pulled out a bottle and two glasses, set them on the desk in front of him, poured two shots of whiskey.

'Drink up,' he said brusquely.

Rick nodded, gulped down the fiery liquid. It brought warmth back into his body, exploding into a hazy heat in the pit of his stomach. Looking directly at the other, he said: 'Be careful, Slim. Lenniger won't be an easy man to hold here in ,jail. It might be that some of his men are still hanging around the territory and they may try to ride in some night and bust him out. And don't forget that there may even be some of the folk in town who might help him if they thought they could get anythin' out of it.'

CHAPTER FOUR

Outlaw Gathering

It was high noon in Hammer Bend as Sheriff Haggerty rode slowly along the main street, eyes flicking to right and left. Not that he anticipated trouble, but since Rick Hartnell had ridden out the previous morning, heading back to the east, there had been an air of rising tension in the frontier town which Haggerty sensed keenly. He did not believe that the outlaw band which Luke Lenniger had led would attempt to return to that part of the territory and bust their leader out of jail, but the possibility was still a nagging thought at the back of his mind, something he could not forget completely and the more he thought about it, the more it began to trouble him.

If those owlhoots did decide to come back to the hills, spurred on by some twisted loyalty to the man who had almost led them to their deaths, then the town would be wide open for them to ride in and shoot it up. He reined his mount outside the saloon, slid from the saddle, swallowing on the dry dust at the back of his throat, then stepped through the batwing doors and into the shade of the saloon. An instant while he stood there, looking around him keenly. It was more an ingrained caution than anything else, born of the days when Hammer Bend had indeed been a wild cattle town. Going over to one of the empty tables, he sat down and rested his elbows on the polished wood. The bartender glanced at him quickly, then moved around the side of the bar, bringing the bottle and glass with him. He set them down on the table in front of the other and hovered there, watching the Sheriff curiously. There was an anticipatory expression on his broad features.

'You look like you're worried about somethin', Sheriff,' he said finally.

There was no answer from the man at the table. It was almost as if the other had not heard the remark. Then he reached for the bottle, tilted it and spilled some of the amber liquid into the glass, lifted the brimming rim to his lips, and drank. Then he quirked a brow at the bartender, still standing there watching him.

'You know what I think, Frank?' he said slowly, running his tongue around his lips.

'No, Sheriff.'

'I think we were wrong about that outlaw gang. I know we've got their leader holed up in the jailhouse, but I figure the others, who were still alive after our attack, didn't ride clear for the border like we expected.'

A moment while the other digested that fact. 'You reckon they'll come back?'

Haggerty nodded slowly, refilled the glass. Heavily, he said: 'I'm sure they will. Once they know that Hartnell is no longer around to help out, they'll ride in and try to get him out of jail before the circuit judge gets here and we have him swingin' from the end of a rope.'

'Don't reckon the judge will be here for another two, mebbe three, weeks.'

'That's right. And we've got to hold him here until then. We can't take the risk of moving him out to Twin Forks. I don't have enough men to help me.'

'You've got your tail in a crack, Sheriff, and no mistake.' The other paused for an instant, then walked back to the bar, slid behind it, wiped it over with the cloth over his arm. Haggerty sat quite still staring directly in front of him. He knew, inwardly, that the other was right. He was responsible for the law and order in this town. It was up to him alone to see that there was no violence, no attempt to get Lenniger out of jail before he could be tried by a jury and sentenced.

There was just the possibility that he was wrong, that the outlaws had been scattered, that the majority of them were south of the border and would remain there until this had blown over. But he didn't think so. They would know that they had been beaten only because they had been taken by surprise and that was something they could guard against in the future. They would have ways of knowing that Rick Hartnell had ridden out of town twenty-four hours earlier and that their most dangerous and implacable enemy was no longer around.

Half an hour later, the bottle on the table was empty and Haggerty rose heavily to his feet, moved a trifle unsteadily towards the door, out into the street. The smell of dust hung thick and heavy in the still air. The piled-up intensity of the sun beat down with a brazen hell-heat on the town. The street itself was virtually deserted. He pushed his sight along it in both directions. A couple of horses stood in front of the hotel on the far side of the street, tethered to the hitching post.

Turning to move towards the office, he paused at the sound of light footsteps behind him. Julie Thompson came hurrying forward. She let her eyes rest briefly on his face, then reached out and touched his arm.

'Is it true that Rick Hartnell has ridden out of town, Sheriff?' she asked.

He hesitated, then nodded. 'That's right, Ma'am. Left yesterday morning just after sun-up. Rode back east.'

He noticed the sudden look on her face. Her eyes were a questioning green in the bright sunlight. 'Do you mind if I talk to you, Sheriff?' she asked.

'About Rick?'

'That's right.' She fell into step beside him on the boardwalk as they walked slowly in the direction of the Sheriff's Office. For a moment, she seemed a little hesitant, as though unsure of herself and he saw a momentary shadow cross her face.

'Do you think that he still hates me for what I said that night my father was shot?'

Haggerty glanced at her in sudden surprise. 'Has he ever said that he hated you?'

'Not with words. But the way he looked, his eyes seemed to tell me that. I thought he was just another gunfighter, a man fast with a gun, handy whenever you need somebody of that calibre to hunt down men like Lenniger. And that callous way he persisted in questioning my father when he knew that he was almost dead.'

'He had to do that, Miss Julie. Don't you see that? We had to know all that your father could tell us if we were to have any chance at all of defeating these killers. Without that information, we could never have caught them on the wrong foot and scattered them as we did. And if we had waited any longer, there was always the chance that they might have ridden down into town and a lot of innocent men and women might have been caught in the gunplay.'

'I realize that now.' She nodded her head slowly. 'I'm sorry for what I said to him that night. I thought he might have remained in town for some time, that he wouldn't ride out like this, without warning, in so much of a hurry.'

'I guess he figured that his work was done and—' Haggerty broke off quickly as he saw the look on her face, the way she stopped abruptly in midstride. 'I'm sorry, Miss Julie. I don't suppose I should have put it like that. But he's a strange man, driven by strange things. I don't think anyone could really understand him, what makes him do the things he does.'

'Perhaps it's because nobody has ever really tried. There always has to be a reason why a man rides a lonely trail, Sheriff, and often it takes a woman to find it.'

In spite of himself, Haggerty gave a quick smile. 'You could be right at that,' he admitted. They were almost at the door of the Sheriff's Office. He paused on the boardwalk.

'Can you tell me anything about him at all, Sheriff?' she asked.

He shrugged. 'What makes you think that I know him?' he countered.

'Because you asked him to come here when you needed someone who wasn't afraid of men like Lenniger. Because you obviously knew the kind of man you wanted and he came without question.'

'You see a lot,' he said slowly. 'Sometimes I wonder about Rick Hartnell. Wonder where he's going and why he seems to be in such a hurry to get there, why he rides alone, and more important, why he harbours such a hatred of men like Lenniger. There are stories, of course, but how true they are, it's difficult to tell.'

'What kind of stories?'

Haggerty lifted his shoulders for a moment, then let them fall. He rubbed the back of his hand over his forehead, blinking his eyes as the glare from the dusty street glinted into them, half dazzling him.

'They say that his family was murdered by a band of renegade Mexican bandits more than fifteen years ago and since that time, he's carried this bitter hatred in his heart against men like that.'

'Perhaps he kills men like this because he wants to.'

Haggerty pondered that, then shook his head. 'No, he isn't like that. This is something he has to do, not because he wants to, because he likes killing, but to avenge the deaths of his family.'

It was almost as though the girl had not heard him. She was, he noticed, staring off into the harsh, brilliant sunlight, but her eyes had softened now and there was a far-away look on her face. Then she drew in a long breath, glanced up at him. 'Thank you for telling me this, Sheriff.'

She flashed him a quick smile, but one tinged with a little sadness that he could not help noticing, then turned away and walked quickly across the street, into the shadows on the other side.

Haggerty watched her closely for a moment, then wheeled and went into the Office, closing the door behind him. Even inside the room, the air was still and stifling. He took a cigar from his pocket, bit off the end, then lit it and inhaled deeply. There was a peculiar excitement in him now as he went along the rear passage to the cells.

Lenniger was standing at the back of the small cell, staring up at the barred window. He turned as he heard the other's footsteps behind him, grinned viciously. Coming over to the door of the cell, he gripped the bars tightly in his fists and peered through them, putting his face close up to the sheriff's.

'Getting scared yet, Haggerty?' he said thinly.

'Nope.' The other puffed hard on the cigar, blowing a cloud of smoke at the outlaw. 'Any reason why I should be, Lenniger?'

'You'll find that out soon enough, lawman. You're a bigger fool than I take you for if you think my men have fled for the border. They'll be around, in the hills yonder, ready to move in and take this town of yours apart.'

'If they are, then I reckon this time we'll be ready for 'em. We smashed you once and we can do it again.' Somehow, Haggerty managed to force conviction into his tone, managed to keep his features straight and unmoving.

Lenniger stared at him through the iron bars for a long moment. Then his lips parted over his teeth. Slowly, he shook his head. 'You're only foolin' yourself and everybody else in town if you believe that. You know that without this *hombre* Hartnell none of the men you have here will dare to go up against my boys when they ride into Hammer Bend.'

Haggerty tightened his lips. 'Reckon you're forgettin'

one thing, Lenniger. If your men do decide to form up and ride into town, you'll be dead long before they can break in these doors and try to bust you out. I'll shoot you dead myself, even though you are a prisoner here, rather than let you escape and terrorise this territory again.'

He saw from the change in the other's expression that the thought had gone home. It had been simply said, but Lenniger recognized that every word had carried the promise of death.

Turning, Haggerty made his way back into the outer office. Although he had tried hard not to show it in front of the other, he was inwardly worried. As the days had gone by since Lenniger's capture, the conviction that perhaps they had been premature in their belief that the outlaw band had been finished when they had shot it up in the hills, had grown within him. If there had been an easy way to get word through to Hartnell, to warn him of his misgivings, he would have done it. As it was, there was nothing definite on which he could base his fears. A moment later he heard the quick tread of heavy feet on the steps outside the office, heard them running up on to the wooden boardwalk. At the first sharp knock, he got to his feet and opened the door.

Dryden, the banker and Doc Thornton stood there, the former looking a bit white and shaky as if he had just heard bad news. Haggerty jerked his head in a curt gesture of admittance and stood aside while they filed into the office. He didn't like Dryden overmuch. The banker was tall and as stringy as a mountain bean, his eyes a watery blue and his whiskers thin and spotty. His long, hooked nose always seemed to have caught too much of the sun, raw and peeling.

'How's Lenniger, Sheriff?' asked Thornton tightly. He lowered himself wheezingly into one of the chairs, casting an apprehensive glance in the direction of the closed door leading back into the cells, almost as if he expected the outlaw leader to appear there at any moment.

Haggerty stared at the others for a moment, his forehead touched with a furrowed frown. He could see a tight bewilderment growing in their eyes and on their faces.

'He's all right, I guess. Still a bit over-confident of himself, but I reckon that's only natural with a man in his predicament. He needs something to bolster up his courage for what's to come.'

'He may have a good reason for being over-confident,' said Dryden abruptly. 'Seems there were a couple of men in the saloon a while back, Haggerty. The bartender swears he recognized them as members of Lenniger's gang.'

'Why wasn't I told about this?' In spite of himself, Haggerty was puzzled at the way his anger flared suddenly against these two men. He said: 'Let's get somethin' straight right now. We've just cleaned up this territory of this gang and we have their leader in jail here awaitin' trial. Ain't no doubt in my mind that once the circuit judge gets here, he's going to hang. If there are still any of those owlhoots around I want to know about it right away.'

He could see the look of fear on their faces changed slowly to one of unveiled hostility, but he didn't care. They were scared and they wanted a scapegoat. Well, better this hostility right from the start. Better they, and he, understand now exactly where they stood. Because it came to him at that moment, that they may be so scared of their own skins, they would rather see Lenniger turned loose right now than have a score of ruthless killers ride into Hammer Bend and shoot the place up, wrecking their vengeance on the townsfolk there.

Dryden muttered defensively. 'Apparently these two *hombres* weren't making any trouble in the saloon, just stepped in for a drink and it wasn't until they were on the point of leaving that the bartender realized who they were.'

Haggerty glanced from one man to the other. He was beginning to understand his anger now, his own abrupt, pointless unpleasantness in the face of what he knew might lie ahead for him – and perhaps the whole town.

'So now you've figured out that sooner or later the whole gang will reform and ride into town to bust their leader out of jail?'

Dryden nodded. 'You've got to admit that it makes a good sense, Sheriff. I don't like this any more than you do. When you went out after that gang and brought Lenniger in, I figured, like most of the others, that this was the end of it. I reckoned he'd be tried and sentenced and we'd hear no more of this whole sordid business.'

Haggerty whirled on him so swiftly that the other seemed to cower back instinctively in his chair. 'But now you've suddenly discovered that you were wrong. You've just found out that there are times when you have to go on fighting if you want to keep law and order and prevent the lawless ones from returning and taking over.' He gritted his teeth tightly for a moment, then controlled his anger with an effort and went on evenly: 'I'm afraid that you've got to find out the hard way that you don't get law and order in a town that has been as wild as this one in the past, without somebody getting hurt.'

'Now you're talking like that *hombre* Hartnell,' muttered Doc Thornton.

'Mebbe so,' answered the other thinly. 'But you didn't just come running here to tell me that the Lenniger gang is probably reforming yonder in the hills. There's somethin' else on your minds. Better speak your piece and get it out.'

Dryden sat up tall and straight in his chair. His features seemed even redder and more flushed than ever. Coldly, he said: 'I think you can visualise what this means to the town if it turns out to be true, Haggerty. It means they'll come to get him out of jail and we don't have the men or the guns to stop them if they do.'

'Then what are you suggestin' that we do about it?' said Haggerty sourly. 'Have you got an answer?'

'Well . . .' The other paused uncomfortably. 'We've

been talking this thing over and—'

'I'll bet you have.' The sheriff's deep voice was deliberately sarcastic. 'And now you've come up with a plan that's going to save the town. Is that it?'

'There's absolutely no call to be flippant about this, Haggerty,' said the banker harshly. 'This is a matter of grave importance to all concerned.'

'Particularly, I guess, for Lenniger.'

Dryden opened his mouth to protest further in the face of the Sheriff's biting remark, then closed it abruptly and looked across at his companion.

Doc Thornton said slowly, 'We reckon there's no problem, Sheriff. We've got to let Lenniger go whether we like it or not. I know exactly what you're going to say, so save your breath, but you have to see this thing from our point of view.' He spoke his last words quickly as Haggerty got savagely to his feet.

'Your way. Damn you both!' Haggerty glared at the two men in front of him. 'You made me Sheriff of this town ten years ago. My job was to keep the peace and maintain law and order here. It wasn't easy, believe me, and the first time that we do manage to clean up the territory of one of the worst gangs of polecats there is, you come crawling in here on your hands and knees, asking that a man like Lenniger, a ruthless killer, one of the worst we know, should go free.'

'It's merely a case of letting one man go so that many others might live,' interjected the banker hoarsely. 'Don't you see that?'

'I can see a lot more than either of you give me credit for,' snapped Haggerty angrily. 'At the moment I can see a couple of yeller-livered cowards who are so frightened that they might get themselves shot up that they're more than willing to go back to the bad old days, to the reign of terror that existed here up to a few days ago.'

Curiously, Dryden did not seem to be touched by this outburst. 'Your insults mean very little to us at this moment, Sheriff,' he said stiffly. 'We're more concerned with saving this town than our own reputations. We have to face the facts squarely whether we like them or not.' Deliberately, he said: 'Can you really imagine what twenty or more ruthless killers could do to a town like this if they rode in?'

'I can guess,' said the other drily. 'Only they're not going to do it!'

'You can't stop them! Except by seeing sense and releasing Lenniger.'

'Never. He's my prisoner and goddamnit, that's the way he's going to stay until that judge gets here.'

For a moment, the banker's face looked extremely worried. Then he uttered a quick, nervous laugh. He said thinly, 'Just one thing wrong with that argument, Haggerty. We elected you as Sheriff of Hammer Bend. Won't take us long to get you out and put in a man who'll do as he's told.'

'Mr Dryden.' Haggertly stared at him inflexibly. 'I've already been warned by Lenniger that his men will soon ride in and take him out of jail. I told him that before I'd allow that to happen I'd walk along that passage yonder and shoot him down myself. That answer is the same for the proposition you've just put forward.'

He saw the two men harden at this and Dryden had an instant answer. 'I've got no personal reason for keeping Lenniger alive. You know that, Sheriff. But how can you pack two different things around in your mind? How can you be two men?'

'I don't get your meaning,' grunted Haggerty. He sat back in his chair, somehow acutely aware of the street sounds outside the building, even though he was still concentrating on the other.

'You would go and shoot down Lenniger rather than see him go free. That's the reaction I'd expect of a lawman and I can understand that and commend you for it. But do you also want to have the blood of half the people in

Hammer Bend on your conscience for the rest of your days; men, women and children? Because that's what will happen if you do as you've just threatened.' He paused and then continued. 'These killers will stop at nothing, you know.' He watched Haggerty with sharp, bright eyes, with a kind of restless attention.

For a long moment, the Sheriff sat silent. Then he leaned forward in his chair and rested his elbows on top of the desk. 'Don't you think we may be all acting a little foolishly? After all, we only have the saloon bartender's word that those were two of the Lenniger gang. Ile could easily have made a mistake. No cause in panicking like this without real reason.'

Dryden tightened his lips, then shrugged. 'Even if you are right, that still doesn't alter the problem. The chance that those outlaws are still around, even though it's remote, is something that we cannot afford to dismiss. This town is wide open. If we are wrong, and they do come, nothing can stop them.'

Doc Thornton leaned forward. 'Don't suppose there might be a chance of getting the circuit judge up here a little sooner, getting the trial over and the sentence carried out before those polecats know anything about it? If the law takes its full course, there ain't no reason why they should blame us for what happens. Like as not, if they're out for revenge then, it'll be this *hombre* Hartnell they'll ride after.'

'Not a chance,' affirmed Haggerty. 'It'll be another two, mebbe three, weeks before he gets here and there's nothing we can do to hurry him along.'

'Then it seems we have no choice.' Dryden got to his feet, took a couple of steps towards the door. Pausing, he looked back to where the Sheriff still sat with his elbows on the desk. 'You still refuse to do as we ask?'

'You mean turn Lenniger loose?' The thick, black brows shot up over the Sheriff's eyes, then lowered into a bar-straight line. 'I sure do. And you'd better not let me see your faces around this jail again unless you've got another kind of proposition to make? Understand?'

'We understand only too well,' snapped Dryden. He stormed out of the office and down the steps, stood in the dust of the street, waiting for Doc Thornton to come out and join him. Almost lazily, but with anger still bubbling and seething inside him, Haggerty pushed back his chair, rose to his feet and walked over to the door, stood there with one arm against the lintel, watching them walk across the street and into the saloon. The doors swung shut behind them and he was on the point of turning back and closing the door when a light step beside him made him glance round.

'I saw Mr Dryden and the doctor leave your office a moment ago, Sheriff,' said Julie Thompson lightly. 'They seemed to be angry at something.'

Haggerty took a cigar from his pocket and bit off the end, made a gesture towards it then placed it between his lips and lit it when the girl shook her head to indicate that she didn't mind if he smoked.

'They came over to ask me to let Lenniger go free,' he said softly.

'To free him!' There was a shocked incredulity in the girl's tone. She stared at him in surprise. 'But why? After all the trouble you went to bringing him in. He's the man who ordered my father to be shot.'

'I know, Miss Julie. But Dryden thinks that the outlaws are still around, that they didn't head out for the Mexican border. If he's right, then they may come ridin' into town, to shoot up the place and bust Lenniger out of jail.'

'And they're afraid that if that happens, a lot of people are going to be hurt. Is that it?'

He nodded, without speaking and stared off along the dusty ribbon of the main street where it led out into the desert to the east. There might still be time to send a man he could trust high-tailing it out there after Hartnell. But now, the other would be somewhere along the desert trail.

'What do you intend to do?' Julie Thompson glanced up at him, her face in the shadow of the parasol she carried.

'I can't let him go. They have to see that. They don't seem to realize that even if I did that, it would be no guarantee that he and his men wouldn't shoot up the town. And at best, we'd be right back where we started. The next time, it wouldn't be easy to take them by surprise as we did the last time.'

One last wave of sunlight broke behind over the hills. Then it faded in a violent splash of crimson as the sun went down behind the hills. The light began to fade slowly now. The reds and greens had gone and it was a new world that lay around Haggerty as he moved out of the small clearing high in the foothills and put his mount to the rocky downgrade. The pines stood in massed shadows around him and the world had turned into a cool, blue, shadowed place with the sharp smell of the pines on the hills in his nostrils and the first little night winds beginning to sigh down the uneven slopes.

He had ridden out from Hammer Bend shortly after high noon, taking the hill trail along which they had brought Lenniger a few days earlier. He had known that he might be heading into trouble, that if the outlaws had come back into the hills, they might spot him while he was several miles away and lay an ambush for him, shooting him down long before he was aware of their presence. But there had been a deep, clinging silence in the hills and the cabin with its bullet-riddled walls and roof stood empty in the clearing. Evidently the outlaws had not returned to this hideout, although that did not rule out the possibility that they may have found themselves another, deeper in the hills. The idea stuck with him as he rode slowly down the trail, among the tall trunks of the trees that stretched up above him and almost completely blotted out the last vestige of daylight.

At this hour, the air suddenly became very thin and clear and the strike of his mount's hoofs ran their echoes straight along the earth, until they reached the tree-line where the deep roots seemed to swallow up the sound. Now that he was in the timber, he traced his way more slowly. Darkness was falling rapidly and the trail, although wide in places, was no longer smooth. Working the down-grade, he approached the valley that lay directly below him, still troubled in his mind about the whereabouts of these outlaws. If only he knew for certain whether they were there on these foothills, or not, he would feel a lot easier in his mind. It made him furious to think that perhaps, after all their planning and fighting, after all that Rick Hartnell had done for the town, it might have been in vain.

The thought of that evoked the hard anger once more and he felt a little tremor pass through him. Had it been wise for him to ride out here in broad daylight where every citizen in Hammer Bend had been able to see him? He had left the prisoner virtually unattended all that time, except for the deputy who had orders to give him his meals and keep a close watch on him. But how far could that deputy be trusted if men like Dryden and Thornton came along and asked for the keys of the cells. After all, the man would be only human if he gave them the keys. Both men were important citizens and there would be no suspicion that they would do anything such as letting Lenniger out of the jail on condition that he gave his word not to wreak vengeance on the town. Men like that, he thought savagely, fiercely, so quick to cheer when Hartnell and he had brought in this outlaw, so easily surrendering now that there was the faintest suspicion of a threat.

He was still in the deep timber when he heard the sound of a solitary rider coming up fast behind him. He paused, turning in the saddle, straining his ears to pick out the sound of the horse, to judge its distance and direction. There was only the one trail in these parts and for a man to be riding as quickly as that he had to be on it. Acting on impulse, something he only half understood, he wheeled his mount, and moved off the trail into the trees, reining the horse and holding his hand gently over its nose to prevent any sound.

The other rider was very close now, spurring his mount at a punishing pace. Whoever it was, he came riding down out of the hills and that made it unlikely that it was one of the townfolk from Hammer Bend. The man came into view, bent low over the saddle, hat pulled well down over his face. Not that it was needed for the darkness was such now that it would have been virtually impossible to pick out the other's features even if he had been riding tall and straight in the saddle with his hat well back on his head.

The thought came to him that his own dust wake must surely have warned the other that there was a rider in front of him and only a short distance away, but the steady abrasion of the other horses's hooves on the trail did not pause, but slowly faded into the night and the distance.

Pushing forward through the trees, he swung back to the trail, let his mount find its own pace for the time being until they hit the main stage route into town. The sense of urgency which had begun to ride him ever since he had discovered that cabin empty, was still there, but he had managed to control it. If Dryden and the others had let Lenniger out of jail, there would be only one thing for him to do. Throw down his badge and leave the town to its own rotten devices. But first, he thought savagely, he'd hunt down the banker and anyone with him and clap them in jail themselves. Then it would be up to the man they got for his job to let them out again. He didn't doubt that they would be able to find somebody more amenable to discipline than himself.

Reaching the main highway, he raked spurs across the flanks of his horse, feeling sorry for it as he did so. It was as tired as he, but the urgency was bubbling up within him again and he knew he had to make it back to town as quickly as possible. Why the mere sight of that solitary rider, heading in this direction from the hills should have disturbed him so, he did not know. But the fact remained, that he had the inescapable feeling that there was something wrong in town, something he ought to know about right away.

There were still lights showing yellowly in the windows of many of the buildings along the main street of town as he rode in at a slow and steady pace. But he sensed a strange silence hanging over the town, something he could not define, but which churned the muscles of his stomach into a hard, tight knot. There was the sound of singing from the direction of the nearest saloon and the tinkling of a tinny piano. As he watched, the doors swung open and a drunk staggered out, stood teetering on his feet for a moment before moving off in an unsteady line along the street, weaving from one side to the other, staring down at the ground under his feet. He did not seem to hear the Sheriff riding up behind him until Haggerty was level with him, then he glanced up, eyes squinting a little as he tried to see who it was.

His lips opened in a faint grin. 'Oh, it's you, Sheriff.' His speech was slurred by the drink.

'That's right.' Haggerty reigned his mount, slid from the saddle. 'Anythin' happened in town since I've been away?'

The other hesiatated, then shook his head ponderously. 'Wouldn't know, Sheriff. I was in the saloon all night.'

Impatiently, Haggerty strode along the street, tethered his mount outside his office. He would get nothing more out of the other, he though fiercely. Best to check on Lenniger. He went inside the darkened office, drew the wooden shutters over the windows, then lit the oil lamp on the desk. Everything seemed to be in order. Getting the keys, he walked over to the other door, stepped into the narrow passage, down to the cells. The dark shape of the man lying on the bunk was clearly visible through the bars.

By the light of the lamp, he saw that it was Lenniger and the other was asleep.

Feeling easier in his mind, he turned and made his way back into the office, sinking into the chair behind the desk and pulling out the whiskey bottle from the drawer, pouring himself a drink. He gulped the raw liquor down in a single swallow and felt the warmth hit his belly as he sat back, relaxing for the first time since noon.

The sound of a rider, racing his mount along the street, reached him as he poured a second glass. For a moment, the sound did not catch and hold his attention for he thought it was just one of the men riding into town. Then a volley of shots crashed in through the window and something larger and heavier followed them and hit the floor in front of the desk as he dived for cover.

CHAPTER FIVE

Threatened Retribution

Haggerty's hand dropped towards his gun but too late for the firing swung away, then stopped and above the crashing echoes there remained only the dull tattoo of hoofbeats fading swiftly into the distance. By the time he had pushed himself heavily to his feet, even that sound had died away completely. He stared about him in numbed surprise. Shards of broken glass were strewn over the floor of the office, glinting in the yellow light from the oil lamp, still miraculously intact.

On the floor, near the desk, lay the heavy stone that had been hurled through the window. There was a tattered piece of paper wrapped tightly around it and as he bent to pick it up, the door swung sharply open and Dryden stood outlined in the opening with a couple of other men behind him, their faces pale, white blurs in the dimness.

'What in God's name happened, Haggerty. We heard shots and then the sound of glass being shattered and came a-running.' He stepped inside and stared about him at the wreckage, eyes widening in surprise.

Haggerty shook his head. 'Reckon some *hombre* wanted to shoot up the Sheriff's Office,' he said, forcing a tight grin. 'If that's so, they certainly picked a funny time to do it.'

'Somebody with a grudge, mebbe?' queried one of the other men. He took a pace forward, noticed the object which the Sheriff held in his hand. 'What's that, Haggerty?'

'Looks like a note of some kind,' muttered the other. He stripped it off the stone and carried it over to the oil lamp, holding it obliquely so that the light fell full on it. He perused it carefully for several moments in silence until, finally, Dryden rasped harshly: 'Well, what does it say, man? Anything important?'

'I reckon so.' There was a sharp edge to the lawman's voice as he turned. 'It's from some of Lenniger's friends. Seems you were right after all, Mr Dryden. They are around someplace, maybe up in the hills, though I searched that canyon and the old shack closely this afternoon and found no sign of 'em.'

Dryden stepped forward and took the note from the Sheriff's hand, read it quickly, then looked up sharply. 'They threaten they'll ride in and finish the town if we don't let Lenniger go peacefully. That's what I've been telling you all along, Haggerty. Are you still going to persist in your foolishness, even in the face of this irrefutable evidence?'

'I've got to, Will. Don't you see that? I'm the man who has to keep law and order and Lenniger is the biggest menace to that there's ever been in these parts. Even if I was to let him go as you want me to, you've got no guarantee at all that these outlaws will keep their word. They'll ride in and shoot up the place the very next day once Lenniger goes up there and tells them how defenceless we are.'

'That's surely a chance we have to take. We can't go on living under the shadow of this threat much longer. We've got maybe two days in which to give our answer and let him go. Then they intend to ride in and take him.'

'Listen to me.' The Sheriff's tone was hard. 'These owlhoots won't shoot up the town because we aren't going to let them. There can't be more than a score of them. We must've killed nearly half of them when we rounded up Lenniger. We've defeated them once, I don't see why we can't do it again, if only we stand together – and this time, we'll be fighting on ground of our own choosing.'

Dryden shook his head fearfully. 'You won't find a single man who'll stand with you. Not this time.'

'Not if I was to get word to Hartnell, bring him back here before those outlaws ride in?' There was a cold, evenness in the Sheriff's voice now and he saw, by the expression on their faces, that he had made his point.

Dryden glowered unbelievingly at Haggerty for a long moment, then his lips tightened. 'There's not a chance of that, Sheriff – and you know it.'

'I wouldn't be too sure about that.' Haggerty moved over to the shattered window. The cold night air blew against his face as he peered out into the street. Here and there, in the shafts of yellow light which spilled from several of the buildings, he could see little knots of people, attracted by the recent shooting. The town seemed tense, danger seemed to have sharpened the senses of the people, making them more like hunted animals than human beings. He realized, for the first time, the razor edge on which this town seemed to be hanging.

Dryden's voice was soft, but touched with a shocked amazement. 'You're not serious, Haggerty. About sending a man after Hartnell and bringing that gunman back to town?'

Haggerty grinned viciously as he turned to face the others. 'You're darned right, I am. If that's the only way I can get this town to stand on its own two feet and fight for what is right, then I'll do that.'

Dryden stood silent for a moment, debating that. Then he shrugged. 'Who're you thinking of sending?'

'I'll figure that out by morning.' Haggerty moved

towards the door, held it open as he stood a little to one side. 'I don't reckon there's anythin' more to be done here tonight. Reckon the town had better get back to sleep.'

'You don't think that gunman will be back?'

Haggerty shook his head. 'He's done all he had to do. He won't be back until he comes ridin' with the other members of the gang. Now get out and leave me to think things out. I've got a lot on my mind right now.'

When the others had gone he closed and locked the door, went back to the desk and sat with his feet up on the desk, turning things over in his mind. It was not only the lawless ones who were determined to nail his hide to the wall, he thought bitterly. Even the most respected citizens of the town would do it if they could. He had pricked their pride, he had shown them that he intended to remain in command here as Sheriff in spite of everything they could do to push him out of this ,job. The star on his shirt gleamed dully in the yellow light from the lamp.

Yawning, he got to his feet, a curious restlessness bubbling up in him. When he had threatened to bring Hartnell back into town, to help him face up to these killers, he had only half-meant it. But the more he debated the possibility, the more it seemed to him that he had no other choice. He was damned if he would stand by and see lawlessness return to the territory just because the people here were scared of the outlaws. He knew that the fact that one man had succeeded in riding into town and shooting up the Sheriff's Office, before riding out again, unmolested, would bring things to a head – and fast.

There was silence in the street outside now. A deep and clinging silence, like the electric tautness which came before the storm, when the thunderheads were piling up on the horizon and the lightning was beginning to flicker across the darkening heavens. The town was a powder keg with a slow burning fuse attached to it. So long as the fuse was long and slow-burning, things would be all right, but he felt sure that very soon, everything would blow up in their faces. The circuit judge could never arrive there in time, even if he managed to get word through to the territorial governor. That would take far too long. The machinery of such a process was far too complicated.

He was on the point of turning in when he heard the call from the cell at the back of the building.

'You still there, Haggerty?'

'I'm here, Lenniger.' He went to the door and opened it, peering along the darkness of the passage beyond.

'Thought I heard a ruckus out there a little while ago.' There was a definite beat of mockery in the outlaw's tone now, something that Haggerty recognized instantly. He felt the white anger beginning to rise within him again, but he succeeded in forcing it down with a conscious effort.

'Some fool tried to shoot up the Office,' he called back. 'Now shut up and get to sleep.'

'Don't reckon there's going to be much sleep for you, or most of the folk in town.' The other gave a bark of mocking laughter. 'Sleep well, Sheriff. This may be the last chance you'll get.'

Bob Travers dragged his spurs across the dusty street, raking up little snakeheads of dust. Rapping with his knuckles on the door of the Sheriff's Office, he threw a quick glance up and down the street, narrowing his eyes against the light of the rising sun, then opened the door and went inside. Taking off his hat, he watched the Sheriff with wary eyes as the other eased his body out of the chair at the back of the desk, rubbing the muscles at the back of his neck. He squinted at Travers, then yawned.

'Glad you got here, Bob,' he said thickly. He turned and sat down again. 'I sent for you, Bob, because you're the only one I can really trust. Besides, they tell me you're one of the best riders in town.'

Travers gave a quick nod, but there was still a puzzled

frown on his face. 'Somethin' on your mind, Sheriff?' he asked.

'I need a little help,' he said. 'I reckon you're the only one who'll do exactly as I say.' Haggerty watched him steadily for a long moment, then nodded as though satisfied with what he saw. 'You heard about the shootin' last night?'

The other nodded, grinning a little as he turned slowly and let his gaze travel around the room. Although most of the debris had been cleaned up, there was still enough remaining to give some indication of the full extent of the damage of the night before.

'They say that those outlaws are gatherin' up in the hills someplace, ready to ride in and tree the town.'

'That's right, Bob. And believe me, they'll carry out their threat, unless—'

'Unless you can get the townsfolk on your side and make 'em stand up to these critters,' suggested the other.

'Right again. I haven't got much support from the others in the town. Even Dryden and Doc Thornton are against me now. They're scared, of course. They know what might happen if the outlaws do ride into Hammer Bend. Could be that they're right. In fact, goddamnit, I know they are. But I reckon that we ought to outnumber 'em when they do come if only I can get these men on my side. There'll be plenty of bullets flyin' around and I need a man who can shoot fast and straight. In short, Bob, I need Rick Hartnell.'

The other looked directly at him. 'But by now he'll be more'n fifty miles away, across the Badlands.'

'I know. That's why I need a fast rider and one who'll do exactly as I tell him. I want you to ride out on Hartnell's trail, keep on ridin' until you find him and bring him back here as fast as you can. In the meantime, I'll do my best to keep these townsfolk under control. It won't be easy. They'll be doing their darnedest to get me to turn Lenniger loose, so as to try to avoid the showdown. But I ain't goin' to do it. Not so long as there's breath in me, and a single slug in my gun for Lenniger.'

'You'd really shoot him down, rather than let anybody turn him loose, Sheriff?'

'That's right, Bob.' There was a deep-seated seriousness in the Sheriff's tone and he looked the other squarely in the face. 'That's exactly what I aim to do. So I reckon the sooner you get mounted up on the fastest horse you can find and bring Hartnell back here, the better it's going to be for everybody concerned. Everybody, that is, except for Lenniger.'

'Sure thing, Sheriff.' The other put his hands on the butts of his guns, then moved quickly towards the door. He paused for a moment, turned, and threw a quick, meaningful glance at the litter on the floor, then flashed a look in the direction of the cells. He noticed the sudden hardness that had come to the Sheriff's face and wasted no further time before running down the steps and into the street.

Three minutes later, Haggerty heard the sound of a fast-running horse go by the office, saw the dust that lifted behind the young rider, settling slowly in the still air. The sun had lifted clear of the horizon now and it promised to be another hot, threatening day.

Travers crossed the river at its lowest point where although it was wide the water was shallow, giving an easy crossing to his mount. The heat of the late morning was a burning pressure on his shoulders and the back of his neck. He had ridden hard through the lush green meadows of the ranches that lay to the east of town, made good time, but now, on this side of the river, as if it had been a sharp dividing line, the country changed. Here lay the grey and burnt-brown of the desertlands where the heat devils danced in the distance and there was an inferno air rolling back from the parched, uneven surface, making a thin, barely-seen turbulence all around him.

The mount seemed to sense the difference, seemed to know that there were many miles of this terrain to be traversed before they came out into the grasslands once more, far to the east, and its pace slowed instinctively. For a moment, Travers debated whether to urge it forward more quickly, then decided against it. He was too good a rider to punish his mount at this early stage. Better to allow it to travel slower and reserve its strength for the task which would face it once they were out in the middle of that burning wasteland.

He rode with a rider's looseness about him, eyes staring keenly ahead, pushing his sight through that shimmering glare, through the brilliance of sunlight heat refracted from the rocks and harsh, white alkali; a limber man with grey eyes half hidden below his lids. Although young, his features had a heavy solidity about them, and there was a hint of quiet, steel-like strength in his body.

When a man had long distances to cover, the best way was the slow and careful way, but he wasn't sure whether Hartnell would be travelling in the same manner. Maybe the other was in a hurry to get back to where he had originally come from.

By high noon, he had covered ten miles, and already the tremendous wash of heat was beginning to tell both on his mount and himself. He crossed the flat bottom of a bone-dry creek from which the water had long since been sucked up into the air. The white stones lay like bleached bones in the shifting sand and he curved around it, rode up the far side of the creek, paused for a moment to allow his mount to blow and shaded his eyes against the glaring sunlight. The desert lay empty before him. There was not a single speck upon it which indicated that men had been there before. He knew now why this was called the Badlands.

Here and there, if a man rode far enough, he would come across the piles of bones that had been picked clean by the buzzards and bleached white by the sun, bones which lay beside the broken wheels of a covered wagon where a party had gone off the trail and become lost in the alkali. This was the price which had had to be paid in the beginning so that the frontier might be pushed westward, pushed clear to California and the clear blue waters of the great Pacific.

Slowly, the flaming disc of the sun curved away to his right, lifting to its zenith and then dipping down at his back, still burning on his shoulders. In front of him, the flat, seemingly limitless horizons were burned a blue-white by it, shivering as though he were looking at them through a layer of water that rippled and shifted in a strange and somehow frightening manner.

It was not until late afternoon that he saw the first sign of life. A small dot on the flatness of the desert, where coarse scrub dotted the rising mounds of rock and dirt. It looked like a small ranch, although he had heard no one mention its presence on this trail. He turned a little in its direction. Perhaps he could get more water and information there, he decided. If Hartnell had passed this way, he had probably had the same idea.

Reining his mount in front of the house which stood some ten yards from the long barn, he sat quite still in the saddle, until the door opened and a man came out on to the porch. He was quite tall, and had a heavy, high-bridged nose and a way of looking at a man as though he were seeing right through him. He brushed the palms of his hands on the blue denims he wore, then stepped down into the dusty courtyard, staring up at Travers, squinting against the sunglare.

For a long moment, the other said nothing, and Travers waited for the invitation to dismount. There was a water trough just at the side of the house and a pipe that led up from some underground well that had been dug at the edge of the courtyard.

The invitation was a long time in coming, but eventually the other said with ill grace, 'Better set down man, and give your horse a drink. Looks as if you've ridden some way.'

'All the way from Hammer Bend,' muttered Travers as he slid from the saddle. He led the sorrel to the trough, let him drink a little, then pulled him away. Too much after so long and hard a ride would make the animal sweat once they started out again and it was better to ride dry than sweat a lot of water, particularly with the night coming up.

'You look as if you're in a hurry to get someplace.' There was a sharp, magpie curiosity in the man's voice as he turned and led the way up on to the porch and then into the house.

The furniture was sparse, looked old, and there was no sign of a woman's hand here, Travers decided. This man lived alone, probably worked this barren land alone for there could be nothing here, in the middle of this wilderness to attract a woman.

'Sit down, mister, and I'll get you a little to eat.' Still the ill grace in the way the other spoke and watched him. Clearly a man who had little company, who saw few men pass this way, for the stage trail ran far to the north of the Badlands and a man had to be in a particular hurry to come this way.

There was also a sharp, distinct tone to the other's words. The syllables were not soft and slurred a little as one would expect from a Southerner. A Yankee from up north, he decided as he lowered himself into the chair at the small wooden table. The other brought out bread and meat, placed them in front of him, together with a mug of hot coffee from the can on the stove.

'Like to offer you puttin' up, but I ain't got no room here and—'

'Thanks for the offer,' cut in Travers, 'but I'll have to dust along before sundown. I'm trying to catch up with a man who came along this trail maybe two days ago. Tall man, lean, little older than me.'

The man turned from the stove, held the mug of coffee in his hand and eyed the other steadily for several seconds before speaking. 'Now why'd you be ridin' after him?' he asked. He seemed to be almost speaking to himself, rather than addressing the other.

'It's important that I reach him as soon as I can.' The other walked over and seated himself in the chair opposite him. He looked harmless in the chair, Travers thought, but the other's eyes were wide open and watchful, speculating on him, keenly and sharply.

'Have you seen any rider heading east along this trail?' Travers applied himself to the food on the plate, chewing thoughtfully, realizing for the first time how hungry he really was.

'Mebbe I have, and mebbe I haven't,' said the other slowly.

'Just what kind of an answer is that?'

'The only answer I'll give until I know why you're trailin' him,' grunted the other. He swilled the coffee down his throat without blinking an eyelid.

Travers shrugged. 'You've heard of Luke Lenniger, I reckon.'

The man's eyes widened just a shade, then he nodded curtly. 'Sure, who hasn't. They reckon he's operating somewhere in the hills to the west.'

'He was. At the moment, he's locked up in the jail in Hammer Bend.'

'You don't say.' There was genuine surprise in the other's voice now, written plainly on his features.

'That's right. And it was this *hombre*, Hartnell, who helped to bring him in alive. Now he's ridin' back east, probably thinkin' that his job's finished. Trouble is that those outlaws are forming up again. They didn't head for the border when they were jumped in the hills and Lenniger was taken prisoner. They've threatened to move in on Hammer Bend and take the town apart if Lenniger isn't set free.'

'So?'

'So the sheriff asked me to ride out after Hartnell and get him back there before there's a wholesale massacre.'

The other wiped the back of his hand over his forehead. The small hairs on his wrists glistened in the sunlight which shafted through the dust-covered windows. Then he nodded. 'He rode past here day before yesterday. Didn't pay much note to him then but now you come to mention it, there did seem to be somethin' about him, somethin' in his eyes that would have picked him out from most other men. So he brought in Lenniger.'

'Alive,' put in Travers. 'I reckon if he'd brought him in dead, there wouldn't have been all this trouble. We'd have put him six feet under the ground on Boot Hill and that would've been the end of it.'

The other was listening to him with the gravest kind of care, his eyes still speculative. He nodded his head slowly from time to time. 'You reckon this man Hartnell will head back to Hammer Bend with you, even if you do manage to catch up with him?'

'I think so. At least, Sheriff Haggerty seemed certain he would.'

'He could be right.' He got to his feet, stood looking down at Travers for a long moment. 'You'll have a hard ride ahead of you if you're to catch him. He's got nearly two days' start on you. That's a mighty long way.'

The afternoon was gone now and with the coming of evening, with the sun dropping down the long slide into the west, the heat head was slowly relieved by the cooler air that swept in from the east ahead of the darkness. The terrain was still flat with here and there, long stretching sand dunes and gulches. To his left, the buttes lifted from the plain, stood out tall and flat-topped, with the last trace of sunlight lying on their crests. His shadow ran before him now, growing longer and longer as the sun went down. When it was gone, he rode on in a blue, cool world, keeping his eyes open, although he did not expect to meet anyone here.

That night, he made camp on a ledge of bare rock that overlooked a broad table of barren wilderness, bony with humpbacked ridges and shot with the darkly shadowed veins of deep gullies in which a horse and rider might fall if they were not sufficiently wary. This was old and useless land, he reflected as he sat beside the fire he had built from small pieces of brushwood, dry as tinder, making a blaze which he knew could be seen for miles in that cold, clear night air. He did not think that anyone might be trailing him, but that was something he kept in mind. Sheriff Haggerty had been afraid of those outlaws in the hills and there was always the chance that they might have sent a small party to trail him if anyone had noticed him leaving town and had guessed his purpose. Like the Sheriff, he had the feeling that more than one of the prominent citizens of Hammer Bend might be in cahoots with the outlaw band, getting information to them.

Far out on the eastern horizon, the setting sun, an hour or so earlier had reflected red rays off a mighty fist of rock which had thrust itself up from the bare desert land. That, he thought, would be Forrester's Peak. Alone and solitary, it was a landmark which stood out from everything for miles around, gave him something definite for which to aim.

The breeze that had picked up during the late afternoon continued until well into the night and flowed cold and unimpeded across the barren face of the Badlands, bringing with it a penetrating cold that soaked into his bones and made him huddle for warmth close to the flickering flames of the fire. He ate a short meal of bread and jerked beef, then got to his feet and hobbled the sorrel.

Going back to the fire, he stretched himself out beside it, lay awake for a long while, listening to the eerie wail of the coyotes off in the distance, and the keening whistle of the wind through the thorn bushes near at hand. After a while, the fire began to die and he reached out and thrust another handful of brush on to it. For a little while, the flames flared up anew, sending redness spreading in a wave over the desert. Then the flames died, but Travers was too tired to reach out for more brushwood and he lay there for a long while in the cold night, thinking of the men and women who might die very soon, back there in Hammer Bend, if he didn't succeed in bringing Hartnell back to town, to help them against these men.

When he woke the next morning, the first grey flush of dawn was just beginning to show in the east, a faint light that brought details into being around him. The cold stiffness persisted in his body as he kicked the embers of the fire into a dull red glow, fed the last of the dry branches on to it, and cooked himself a meal.

He ate quickly, anxious to be on his way once more. The short dawn was almost over when he finally saddled up and rode out over the flat plateau and down on to the narrow trail. Behind him, a faint grey wisp of smoke from the fire he had kicked out still hung in the air but it was fading rapidly. Once again, as on the previous day, the heat head rose swiftly in intensity as soon as the sun came up and it was virtually impossible for him to shield his eyes against the savage glare as he rode directly towards it. His mount was still bearing up under the punishing pace he set, but there would be another day before he crossed this stretch of alkali and even when he reached the other side, there was no way of telling how long it would be before he found fresh signs of Hartnell's trail and managed to run him to earth.

The temperature rose quickly throughout the next hour until he guessed it was well over a hundred and ten. There was no shade anywhere along this open trail and the heat stayed with him, bringing the sweat out of his body, soaking into his shirt until it stuck to his limbs, chafing and irritating where the caustic grains of alkali dust had worked their way into the folds of his skin.

He ate another quick meal shortly after high noon, pushed on towards the hills that now showed up in the distance ahead of him. The sun burned on him, the glare from the ground worked its way through lowered lids and etched itself redly into his brain. It was impossible to shut it out, impossible to even draw a breath that did not hurt in his lungs. He passed the shattered remains of a covered wagon at the side of the trail, the pitiful belongings strewn on the ground where death had overtaken some family at this point when they were on their way across the face of the continent in search of a new life in the lush green lands of California.

One had only to ride this desert trail to discover for himself the terrible cost in lives which had been paid in the past so that the country might expand and the new lands be exploited to the full. Someday in the future, he thought reflectively, there might even be a railroad built across this waste land, the gleaming metal rails laid in the sand and alkali, the trains carrying people across the country far more quickly than was dreamed of now.

He shrugged, tried to think of the task in hand. He recognized that his thoughts were wandering only so that he might take his mind off the heat and the discomfort. Hartnell was a fool to return by this route, he thought. Any man in his senses, if he were no longer in any real hurry, would have taken the stage trail to the north, where it ran between tall forests of pine, with the sharp smell of needles in the air and cool green spaces under the trees.

The previous day, when he had first ridden into the desert, he had been nagged by the feeling that perhaps this was just what Hartnell had done, that he had decided to return east by the stage trail. But now that the fact that this was the trail he had taken had been confirmed by the man back there at that isolated ranch, he felt a little easier in his mind.

It was shortly before sundown that he turned in the saddle, looked back to where the great red flare of the setting sun painted the sky behind him, and spotted the small band of riders in the distance. They were little more than a tightly bunched group of black dots, picked out only because they were then on the point of heading down a rise on the horizon and the sunlight was directly at their backs. He could make out the dust raised by their passage quite easily, knew that his eyes had not deceived him; and that these men, whoever they were, were riding up fast on his trail.

At the rate they were travelling, he guessed that they would catch up with him before nightfall even if he pushed his tired mount to its utmost limit. Swiftly, he cast about him for an cover. The nearest was the rocky entrance to the foothills less than two miles away. Bending swiftly over his mount's neck, he gigged it with the spurs, felt it leap forward, breaking into a quick run.

Some instinct told him that those men behind him were not inclined to be friendly. Haggerty would not send anyone after him and that left only one other possibility. His leaving town had been noticed and word had been passed on to the outlaws waiting in the hills. They had clearly decided that he must be stopped at all costs from reaching Hartnell and this group had been sent after him to make sure that he didn't succeed.

Half an hour later, he was still almost a mile from the hills and the men on his trail were gaining rapidly. Their mounts seemed to be fresher than his own and there seemed little doubt that he had been seen. On that flat expanse of white alkali, it would have been difficult not to have spotted him. Those men had the sun at their back and under those conditions it would be possible to see for miles.

By now, his mount was tiring rapidly, stumbling now and again in the shifting alkali. Some of the white dust must have worked its way into the animal's hoofs for it was beginning to limp a little. The distance between his pursuers and himself had closed to less than a quarter of a mile and although it was almost dark, they would be able to follow him easily now, even in the foothills. His only chance lay in slipping from the saddle and taking cover among the rocks where he might be able to use his rifle to good advantage before they were able to take him from three sides.

The desert ahead made a slow turn into the darker, rocky country. Kicking the sorrel's flanks, he urged it forward. A moment later, he heard its hoofs strike the hard surface of rock, knew that he had made it by the skin of his teeth and had only a few yards to go. A volley crashed out from behind him. It fell short, but he knew that the next would be closer.

The thunder of hoofs sounded loud in his ears as he rode swiftly into the dark rocks, eyes alert. The trail wound in and out of the rocky outcrops here, twisting and turning seemingly endlessly. He put his horse to a steep incline, reached a sharp bend in the trail, then slid from the saddle, whipping the high-powered Winchester from its scabbard as he did so, rushing for the shelter of the rocks. His horse ran on for several yards into the darkness before stopping.

Crouching down, he peered into the dimness ahead of him. He could just make out the four riders now as they rode quickly forward, leaning low in their saddles. Evidently they were suspicious, had guessed he had gone to earth somewhere near by and were not making the mistake of riding into a trap. They reined their mounts some twenty yards from the rocks, circled around for a moment, then swung down to the ground, grabbing their rifles as they snaked their way forward. One man, who seemed to be the leader, gestured with his left hand, urging the others to spread out and not to move forward in a tight bunch.

Another volley crashed out and there was the thin, high-pitched whine of lead striking the rocks and shrieking into the distance in murderous ricochet. Travers pulled his head low in reflex motion, pressed himself hard against the rock, steadying the rifle in front of him. He could make out one of the men as the others eased his way around the base of the rocks in a wide circle, evidently determined to outflank him and take him from behind. Travers made a quick guess as to distance and elevation, drew a thoughtful sight on the dark blob of the man's head as he slithered around. He waited patiently and took up the trigger's slack, finger bar straight, waited until he had the outlaw's shoulders in the notch of his sights.

The man moved into an open stretch, could be clearly seen even against the jumble of rocks. Travers squeezed the trigger and let go a single shot, saw the man suddenly throw up his arms and stagger back before dropping out of sight completely. He knew from the way the other fell that he had been hit.

'He's up there, over to the right!' The hoarse voice sounded from the rocks a little way in the distance below Travers. He tried to judge where it had come from, but there were little echoes here and it was difficult to tell for certain and he didn't want to risk a second shot without a proper target for fear of giving himself away completely. They may not have spotted his muzzle flash the first time; but they would certainly do so when he fired again.

The man yelled more orders. There was the hard scrape of a boot on the rocks and Travers swung round sharply. The sound appeared to have come from his left, and almost on a level with him, damnably close.

Moving slowly, an inch at a time, he wriggled sideways, worming his way into a deep crinkle in the rocks where there had been a geological upheaval at some time in the distant past, leaving this fold in the ground. He could pick out the sounds of the three men as they worked their way towards him, but they were keeping their heads down, their bodies out of sight. Evidently they were used to this kind of thing, did not intend to expose themselves now that they knew approximately where he was holed up and that he was alert and watchful.

Somewhere, he heard a horse snicker softly, wondered with a part of his mind if it was his own. The darkness was almost absolute now and no matter how he tried to pierce it with his vision, he met nothing but a jumble of angled contours that made little sense and nothing seemed to move among them although he knew that the remaining three killers must be very close to him now.

They had the advantage that they knew where he was and could approach him from three sides, take him without him knowing where they were. The horse snickered again, to his left and he swung his head sharply, fingers tightening on the rifle in his hands. He lifted it gently, resting it on the smooth, flat rock in front of him, careful not to make too much movement.

Something was spooking that horse, he decided and it could only be one of the outlaws. For several seconds, he could hear nothing but the thudding of his own heart against his ribs and the blood beginning to pound through his veins. Then he caught the sudden movement at the very edge of his vision. It had been so slight that had he not been watching with averted vision, he might have missed it altogether but it came again a split second later and he made out the dark figure of one of the men creeping over the flat top of one of the rocks.

He sucked in a deep breath as he focused his attention on the other. Either the man was plumb crazy moving in the open like that, simply asking for a bullet in his head, or he was deliberately showing himself like that, keeping the other's attention fixed on him while his two companions worked their way quickly forward in other directions.

Releasing his breath in small, sharp pinches, he brought the rifle to bear on the man. This might be a dead giveaway as far as the other outlaws were concerned, but at least it would reduce the odds a little more and at the moment, three-to-one were just too high for him.

Gently, he squeezed the trigger, felt the rifle buck in his hands, knew even as the sharp report sounded in his ears that he had aimed true. The man paused and for a moment, it was as if the bullet had missed. Then the other began to slide sideways, slithered over the smooth top of the rock, until he reached the edge, then went over, falling perhaps ten feet before his limp and broken body hit the ground below. The man bounced, and rolled, then ceased to move.

Reaction was immediate. He ducked his head sharply as bullets spattered the rocks around him, striking within an inch of his head. The flash of the rifle had been spotted instantly by the others and now they were pouring lead into his hiding place from all angles.

The firing continued for the best part of a minute, then stopped. He reckoned that the other two men had paused to reload their weapons. Straining his eyes, he tried to pick them out in the gloom, trying to judge the direction from which their fire had come. But he could see nothing.

Then, a moment later, a voice yelled harshly: 'You don't stand a chance, mister. Better throw out your guns and step on to the trail with your arms hoisted. We don't want to kill you, but we will if we have to.'

He remained silent, knowing that it was a trap. These men would never let him leave this place alive. He had killed two of their companions and for that he would have to die. The moment he stepped out into the open, even though he threw out his guns, they would shoot him down.

'We ain't goin' to ask you again,' shouted another voice, reaching him from a slightly different direction. The echoes broke on the rocks all around and it was impossible to place the source of the original sound. 'We've got no quarrel with you. Only with the man you're trying to find. Throw out your weapons, then you can mount up your horse and ride on back the way you came.'

'Come on up and try to get me,' he called back. 'Two of

you are finished and I reckon I can pick off the rest of you.'

A bullet smashed against the rocks near him and he pulled himself sideways, swearing a little under his breath. That had been a trifle too close for comfort.

'All right, buster, you asked for it!'

Crabwise, keeping his head well down, he scuttled around the sheltering rocks, crouched low while he threw a swift glance about him, considering his position, then moved on again for another couple of yards before throwing himself down behind a low overhang. He heard the clatter of boots on the rocks near the place he had just left, followed by the sharp bark of a sixgun. Then there was the dull mutter of voices, more movement, and he knew they had rushed his last position and were now preparing to move after him now they had discovered he was no longer there. They were swinging round, separating, trying to box him in. He edged back and saw his danger at once. This narrow canyon into which he had moved was a dead end, there was no escape from it. Whether or not those two men had known this, or whether it had been just intuition on their part, he did not know, but a second later, one of them called: 'We've got you trapped now. Why not act sensible and give up?' The sound of the voice was thinned and short and he heard the tight rattle of brush just beyond the huge rock that stood at the end of the canyon.

Gently, he laid the rifle down, pulled the Colts from their holsters and stood with his back pressed hard against the smooth stone, eyes narrowed, unfocused, taking in everything in front of him. Here, it was doubtful if they would be able to attack him from the rear. They would be forced to come on him from the front and at least he stood a chance that way.

For long moments, nothing moved. Silence lay over the rocks. He guessed that the others were trying to outwait him, hoping that he would break first and give himself away by the need for air, for movement. He thinned his lips grimly. He'd be damned if he'd fall for that. Patience made him stand rock steady and he knew he could outwait these men. Outlaws were not renowned for their courage unless they held the advantage of numbers and two to one were short odds for these killers, especially now that he had shown himself to be handy with a gun.

They would take their time, keep their eyes open and move cautiously before trying anything. Perhaps they would try to come at him from two directions at the same moment.

Even as the thought passed through his mind, there was a sudden movement in front of him and the dark shadow of one of the men stepped swiftly into the open, pulled up his gun and fired. The crash of gunfire almost deafened him as the echoes rolled around in the confined space of the narrow canyon. The slug tore a deep furrow along his left arm, sending a deep stab of pain into his shoulder, so that he almost dropped the gun he held. Abruptly, he fought for control, sucked a gust of air into his body, forced his vision to clear and fired twice in rapid succession. Whirling just as the outlaw's gun flamed again, he dropped sideways, releasing the thumbed-back hammer of his gun. The outlaw had moved a couple of paces into the canyon, certain that his bullets had found their mark, that Travers was dead on his feet. He paid the price of his folly a moment later as the slug took him full in the throat, pitching him forward, his gun flaming into the earth at his feet as he fell, the slug whining off into the distance. Freezing all motion for the briefest part of a second, Travers got in another shot as the man hit the ground, making certain this time that he was dead.

Then he swung about sharply, looking for the other, knowing that the last outlaw was around someplace, ready to move in. He had been so sure that both men would come at him together that the fact that only one man had stepped out into the open had come as a surprise to him. For a moment, he felt completely off balance. Abruptly, he righted himself, forced steadiness into his body and mind.

The sudden sound at his back warned him of the danger there, but even as he whirled and threw himself sideways, he knew he would be too late to stop the man who had crept up on him unobserved, from squeezing off that one shot which would kill him. The man stood atop the smooth wall of the canyon. Evidently he had worked his way around and climbed the steep side, coming up at Traver's rear.

Almost, the other's ruse worked. The outlaw had been expecting him to whirl and fire in the same instant, had lined up his gun on Traver's back. The sudden sideways movement took him by surprise. Travers felt the slug tear his leg as he went down, raking a bloody furrow along it. Then he was on the ground, the blow of striking it sending a jarring shock of agony lancing up into his body. All of the wind seemed to have been knocked out of his lungs and it was as if his chest had been caved in by a mighty blow. Fiercely, he fought to hold on to his consciousness. He knew that the other was moving in, steadying himself for another killing shot and that this time, the killer would make no mistake.

With an effort, he managed to bring up his gun, squeeze the trigger with a jerk. The outlaw, moving forward with a grim purpose stopped suddenly and let out a harsh bellow of pain. The gun dropped from his fingers as the bullet smashed along his forearm. With a bellow of rage, he lunged forward, throwing himself at Travers.

There was no time for him to duck or to roll out of the way. The toe of the outlaw's boot caught him on the side of the head. Lights flashed in front of his eyes and for several seconds, he lay there unable to move, a great roaring in his head. Savagely, he forced himself to move, to push his hands behind him and twist sideways on the rocks, knowing what was coming next, knowing that this man would fight dirty like all of the others.

The blow aimed at the small of his back missed by an

inch and the other's foot struck the hard rocks. He heard the savage curse that broke from the man's lips as the pain jarred into his leg. Squirming, Travers pushed himself to his feet, stood swaying unsteadily for a moment, his back and shoulders against the wall of the canyon, trying to force away the dull, sick pounding in his ears, the flashing haze that danced tantalisingly in front of his vision.

Through tear blurred eyes, he saw the other draw himself slowly up to his full height, move purposely towards him, his arms swinging by his sides, his lips twisted into a thin sneer, eyes glittering with the killing fever.

CHAPTER SIX

Sixgun Trail

The outlaw charged in, arms swinging wildly. He made no attempt to go for the gun that lay somewhere among the loose rocks at his feet. Travers swung his right hand, his fist hit rock-hard flesh as it grazed the point of the other's jaw, but the blow did not stop the man as he bored in, grunting under his breath. His bunched fist struck Travers on the chest, seemed to capsize his lungs, to crush his ribs. He felt the air rush out of his body. There was a fire in his chest as he tried to stand upright, giving ground a little as he slid his body along the canyon wall. There was a high-pitched ringing in his ears that refused to go away and he knew that the slug which had torn along his arm and the other in his leg, although not seriously wounding him, had caused him to lose some blood, had slowed up his reactions to the danger point.

He knew instinctively that the other would settle for nothing short of his death now. Stubbornly, he dug in his heels and waited, saw the other shake his head a little as if to clear it, then move in again, but the outlaw telegraphed his side-swinging punch and Travers was able to step inside it, driving his fists with all of his strength into the other's throat, just below the adam's apple.

The killer grunted, staggered back with a bleat of pain,

hands going up to his throat as the vicious, chopping blows threatened to paralyse the muscles there, making it difficult for him to breathe properly.

Travers hit him with another piston stroke as hard as he could, then stepped a little to one side expecting the man to fall, to pitch forward and hit his head on the rocks. But the other merely blinked his eyes and swayed, still on his feet, lips still drawn back over his teeth in an animal snarl of hatred and anger.

Lumbering forward once again, his breath wheezing in and out of his barrel chest, the other suddenly lunged forward, taking Travers by surprise, throwing him completely off balance as he thrust with all of his weight, getting his arms around the other's chest, pinning his hands to his sides, locking fingers in the small of his back and squeezing in a bear hug that threatened to force Travers' spine back until it snapped under the inexorable pressure like a rotten twig. He gasped savagely as he tried to prevent the other from bending him backward, knowing that the human spine could only take so much and would then snap.

The thick arms tightened their grip in spite of everything he could do and the hard rock at his back prevented him from moving under the other's weight. Pain jarred in agonising waves through his body and he felt himself being suddenly lifted off his feet, knew that it was only a matter of moments before he was finished, with his back broken. Fighting to keep a hold on his buckling consciousness, he went suddenly limp, heard the sudden grunt of satisfaction from the man who held him, knew that the other figured he had finished him. For a fleeting second, as he allowed himself to slump fractionally to one side, the terrible pressure around his body eased and he suddenly jerked his arms free, brought up his elbows and rammed them with all of his strength into the man's chest, then brought up on knee into his groin.

With a savage cry of anger and pain, the other reeled

back, head lowered a little as he tried to protect himself from any further attack on the vital parts of his body. Even as the other staggered back Travers hooked one foot behind the outlaw's ankle, jerked quickly. The man uttered a thin, strangled yell and fell against the far side of the canyon, arms flailing helplessly as he strove to maintain his balance.

Jerking and twisting, he managed to prevent his head from striking the solid rock and took the fall on his shoulders instead. Although the fight was temporarily in his favour, Travers found himself unable to take full advantage of the fact. All of the strength and feeling seemed to have been drained from his body. There was a roaring in his head, a throbbing ache at the back of his temples and for a moment he felt consciousness flickering. In the gloom, he glimpsed the other's face wavering like a grey blur in the darkness, something he could not focus properly.

The other remained on his knees for a long moment and it was not until Travers dropped his gaze that he realized why the man had not risen while he had had the chance to move in for the kill. His right hand had been searching among the loose rocks that littered the floor of the canyon, fingers scrabbling wildly. Now they had found what they were looking for, had closed around the butt of the revolver which had fallen there when Travers's bullet had raked the other's forearm.

Slowly now, the other drew himself up to his full height. His teeth showed whitely in the shadow of his face. He stepped forward a pace and lined the gun on Travers's chest.

'This is where you get it, cowboy,' he grated. 'I warned you back there to throw in your hand and move out, but you refused to take that chance. Now you're finished and it won't be long before Hammer Bend goes the same way.'

For a moment, Travers measured the distance of the other with his eyes, debated whether there was a chance at all of reaching him before he could pull that trigger, knew with a sickening sense of loss that there wasn't a chance in the world. Tensely, he braced himself for the sudden report, for the smashing impact of lead as it tore into his body and wondered vaguely what it would be like to die, only sorry at that moment that he had failed in his task.

The sharp report hammered against his ears. For a moment, he stood there, absolutely still, scarcely aware of the fact that he had not been hit, that the man in front of him had unaccountably missed. Then he saw the outlaw begin to sway forward, the gun in his hand unfired, already slipping from fingers that no longer had the strength to hold it.

He had trouble standing straight and when he did move forward, his ankles rocked as if they lacked the strength to bear his weight. The brutal beating he had just taken had left him numb in both mind and body. Then he blinked and forced himself to look round, saw the man who came into the entrance of the canyon, the Colt held rock steady in his right hand. For a moment, the other glanced down at the dead outlaw, touched him with the toe of his boot, then thrust the Colt into its holster and turned.

'Looks as if I got here just in time,' he said pleasantly. He came forward and took Travers's arm and quite suddenly, focusing his eyes on the man in front of him, Bob Travers knew that this was the man he had ridden across that terrible desert to find.

'I'd made camp back yonder in the hills when I heard the shootin' and decided to come over for a look-see.' Hartnell grinned at the other as he fastened the rough bandage around Travers's arm. 'Looked to me though as if you didn't need much help. You seem to know how to take care of yourself with a gun.'

'I guess they were all too sure of themselves,' muttered Travers. He squatted by the fire which Hartnell had built in a small hollow, letting the warmth soak into him. 'Except for that last one. He was the tricky one.'

Hartnell nodded. 'You say you were ridin' out to look for me. Somethin' happened back in Hammer Bend?'

'I guess you might call it that,' nodded the other. He sipped the scalding hot coffee from the mug in front of him. 'Those outlaws you scattered. They've ridden back into the territory. They didn't head south for the border as you figured they would. One rode into town a couple of nights back and shot up the Sheriff's Office, tossed in a note that they were going to ride into town and shoot up the place if they didn't turn Lenniger loose.'

Hartnell's face was suddenly grim, the lips pressed tightly together. He stared off into the darkness of the rocks for a long moment before speaking. Then he said harshly: 'I had a sneaking suspicion that might happen. What does Haggerty feel about it?'

'He sent me after you to try to get you to ride back with me. The townsfolk, particularly Dryden the bank manager and Doc Thornton are agitatin' for him to let Lenniger go free. They reckon that these critters will keep their word if they do that.'

'Not a chance in hell,' grunted the other. He stirred the twigs with his toe, sent the sparks flying high into the air. 'They'll ride in and take over the town, lock, stock and barrel and before the townsfolk know what has hit 'em, they'll be working for these outlaws. That's what Lenniger has been waitin' for all this time. If we hadn't stopped him when we did, he would have been running Hammer Bend by now and nobody would have been able to do a darned thing about it.'

'Then you will ride back with me?'

'Sure. This is somethin' that has to be finished, one way or the other.'

'When do we ride?' Travers heaved himself painfully to his feet.

Hartnell shook his head. 'Better rest up for a couple of

hours. That arm of yours will be giving you hell pretty soon and the more you can rest it, the better. Besides, there's still plenty of the night left for riding. Bed down by the fire for a while and we'll ride out in an hour or so. I'll wake you when it's time to move out.'

Gratefully, the other stretched himself out on the bare rocks beside the fire, rolled over on to his side, easing his bruised body into a comfortable position. Hartnell moved a little distance away, sat on an outcrop of rock, his body in the shadows, beyond the red circle thrown by the flickering flames. He sat for a long while, gazing thoughtfully into the dimness around him. Overhead, the sky was clear, the air thin and cold and the stars burned like flames in the velvet vault of the heavens, seeming to be so close that he had only to lift up one hand to be able to touch them. A little while later, the moon rose in the south-east, round and full and white, throwing long, black shadows among the gullies. Around him, there were the usual night sounds of the desert. The dismal, undulating wail of a coyote, rising and falling along a saw-edged scale.

After a while, he rose stiffly to his feet, feeling the coldness in him and placed a can of coffee over the fire, kicking at the embers with the toe of his boot. His companion, he noticed, was still sunk in deep, exhausted sleep. He guessed that the other had ridden hard these past two days in the hope of catching up with him, could have had little sleep the night before, and the brutal beating he had taken from that dead outlaw lying in the gully would have sapped most of his remaining strength. But if they were to get back to Hammer Bend before those outlaws carried out their threat, he could not afford to let him rest too long, no matter how much he would have liked to, no matter how much the lad needed that rest. The journey was going to be a bad one. It would help if they could make good time during the night when the air was cool and they did not have the burning light of the sun in their faces.

He lifted the mug of coffee to his lips, sipped the scalding liquid. For a further five minutes or so, he sat there in silence, watching the lift of the hills around him, then he got to his feet and walked over to where Travers lay stretched out on the earth. Gently, he shook the other by the shoulder, saw the eyes flick open instantly, alert, like those of an animal, ever ready for danger.

Travers sat up, wincing a little as pain jarred through his stiff limbs.

'Time to be movin' out,' said Rick softly. 'Better get some of this coffee inside you, though. It'll bring a bit of warmth back into your body and you'll need it. We've got a long, hard ride ahead of us.' He grinned lop-sidedly at the other. 'Guess I don't have to tell you that after what you've been through these last two days.'

Travers gave a quick nod, rubbed the muscles at the back of his neck with his fingers, then accepted the mug which Rick held out to him, drank it slowly, running the liquid around his mouth before swallowing it. When he had finished, he got unsteadily to his feet, stood for an instant, staring about him.

'You reckon you can make it?' asked Rick solicitously.

The other nodded slowly. 'I'll be all right once we've saddled up and we're moving. Besides, we've got to get back in time. No tellin' when those coyotes will ride against the town.'

Rick poured the rest of the coffee over the fire, killing it. In the moonlight, it was possible to see for some distance now and as they climbed into the saddle, Rick swung his arm to the east.

'We'll take that trail,' he said slowly. 'There's no waterhole all the way across the desert there, but it's the shortest route and if we're to get to the town in time—'

Travers nodded to indicate that he understood. His grip on the reins was a little tighter than normal, but that was the only indication of the pain which was still in his body.

*

When Sheriff Haggerty walked into the saloon at the corner of the intersection there was evidence that, although it was still only nine-thirty at night, the place was closing up. The girls were trooping up the wide stairway and the bartender was already mopping the top of the bar and placing the bottles back under the long counter. He straightened up sharply as the Sheriff walked in, then gave him a brief nod. Haggerty had a sense of being baulked even as he walked out to the bar but he gave no outward sign of his feelings as he leaned up against the counter.

Through the wide crystal mirror at the back, he was able to keep an eye on the other men still there in the saloon. A handful still sat at the round tables, some playing stud poker, others drinking, talking in subdued whispers among themselves. Everywhere, he could sense that strange and indefinable air of tension which had been growing in town all day until it had almost reached its flash point. He knew inwardly what it signified. Things were rapidly coming to a head and unless he played his hand real well, things might get out of control. He wondered tensely whether Travers had succeeded in the task he had set him, whether he had managed to catch up with Rick Hartnell. He did not doubt that the other would return with him once he was acquainted with the position in Hammer Bend. But he had ridden out two days before Travers had left and a man could travel quite a distance in that time, even across such terrible country as the Badlands.

If Travers hadn't found him, then they were in real trouble. He knew he could not hold off the insistent Dryden for long and now that word had got around concerning the real cause of the shooting outside the jailhouse, more and more of the influential citizens were tending to associate themselves with the banker. It would not be long, he decided, before they had formed themselves into a delegation, coming to demand that he do as the outlaws had demanded and let Lenniger go free.

So very soon the lines would be drawn and it would all be over – finished. Either he would have his way and these people would be forced to recognize that they too had a duty to perform if they wanted this town to remain clean and free from outlawry and corruption – or he would have killed Lenniger in that small cell at the back of the jail-house and the town would be shot up by the vengeful outlaws.

Wryly, he was forced to admit that he would have to take the latter course. He did not relish the idea of shooting down even a man like Lenniger in cold blood, an unarmed man. Had he been a man filled with hate like Rick Hartnell, he might have done it. But he knew that if it came to the point, he would go through with it.

'You want a drink, Sheriff?' The bartender had stepped over and was looking across the bar at him.

Haggerty nodded. 'Whiskey,' he said shortly, took the bottle and glass which the other pushed over to him, then called the other back as he made to move away.

'You closing early tonight, Lem?'

'That's right, Sheriff.' The other's tone was defensive, as if he expected some argument, and knew he hadn't any answer to offer.

'Why?'

'Ain't got many customers tonight. The town's on its toes. You must have felt it too, Sheriff.'

'Sure, I've felt it. They're all scared. They know that things are coming to a showdown pretty soon and that it only needs a little push and a lot of men are going to die. Trouble is, Lem, that they don't recognize what will happen if they give in now. We finished that outlaw band a little while ago. We've got their leader locked away in one of the cells and—'

'But how long can you keep him there, Sheriff?' muttered a hoarse voice at his back.

Haggerty did not turn but studied the other's reflection in the mirror behind the bar.

'I reckon I can keep him there long enough for the circuit judge to bring him to trial, Doc,' he said, then glanced around as Thornton moved to one side of him and leaned against the bar.

'You're only fooling yourself, Haggerty.' The other shook his head. 'The town won't let you sacrifice it, just to please your own vanity and sense of justice.'

The Sheriff thinned his lips, then controlled himself with an effort. When he spoke again, his tone was tight, but even. 'Is that why you reckon I'm keeping him in jail, Doc? For once, be honest with yourself.'

'I don't need to look to my own actions for justification,' snapped the other. He reached out a hand for the whiskey bottle, filled a glass and tilted it to his lips, downing it in a single gulp, shaking his head a little as the raw liquor hit the back of his throat. 'I want to see law and order prevail just as much as you do, but I'm not prepared to have forty, maybe fifty, men and women killed for it.'

'There ain't any reason why they should be killed. Somebody had to fight when this town was first built. Indians and then the renegade soldiers from the war and finally these outlaws. We licked 'em once, up there in the hills, on the ground of their own choosing. Now we've got the chance to wipe 'em out altogether and we can do it if everybody is willin' to throw in his hand with me. If we all go around actin' like a bunch of scared rabbits, then they'll ride in and tree the town. But if we stand up to them, we outnumber them by three-to-one.'

'We're not gunfighters, Sheriff. You know that. There aren't many men in town who've handled a gun against other men, even outlaws.'

'Then it's time they learned that they've got to sacrifice somethin' if they want this town to go on living.' Haggerty studied the other closely, remembering that it was Thornton and Dryden and a few of the other leading citizens who had elected him to office, promising all the help he needed in his battle to bring law and order to a town that verged on lawlessness. He knew instantly that it would be useless to remind the other of those promises.

He said deliberately: 'I've sent a man out after Rick Hartnell. With luck, he ought to have caught up with him by now and they'll be ridin' back into town any hour now. When he gets here, he might get some of you to see a little sense. All of this talk of letting Lenniger go and—'

'You're wrong, Sheriff.' There was a faint note of hopelessness in the other's voice. 'We knew that you'd sent Travers out after Hartnell. He took the desert trail, didn't he?'

'That's right. Sure he did. So what?'

'Only that Hewitt, on the stage yesterday, spotted a bunch of men riding out of the hills. He swears they are part of the Lenniger gang, even though he only caught a quick glimpse of them, figured they might be settin' to rob the stage, but they went clean by him and took the desert road.' He lifted his thick brows a little. 'Hate to disillusion you like this, Sheriff. But it seems pretty clear to me that they knew about Travers and they were headed after him. They stand a better chance of catching him than he does of reaching Hartnell in time.'

'You ain't got no proof they were after Travers,' grunted Haggerty thickly. Even though he tried to keep the doubt out of his voice, he had to acknowledge himself that it was probably true. This was what he had feared and now it seemed that it had happened; that the outlaws had been watching the eastward trail over the desert, just in case he did try to get word through to Hartnell.

'What more proof do we need, Sheriff?' Thornton's tone was bland. 'Hartnell hasn't arrived back here, has he? And if Travers had ridden hard all night, he would have brought him back a couple of hours ago. Seems you've lost out on this one, Sheriff.' He finished his drink, moved away from the bar. 'The town's mighty quiet. Reckon most of the folk have got something on their minds.'

Haggerty watched him as he walked out of the saloon. The batwing doors had barely closed behind him when they opened again and he saw Julie Thompson standing there on the boardwalk. Her gaze travelled over everyone there, then rested on him. She made a little gesture with her hand.

Finishing his drink, he went outside. The street was quiet now and almost deserted. As Thornton had said, the town was waiting for something. It was like the hush before the breaking of the storm and he felt a little tremor pass through him as he looked down into the girl's face.

Curiously, she did not seem to be frightened like most of the others. Her lips were pressed together, but steady.

'What is it, Miss Julie?' he asked quickly, lowering his voice a little.

She threw a quick glance over her shoulder, then said: 'I thought I ought to warn you, Sheriff. Dryden is over at the other saloon, talking to a bunch of men. The way he's talking, I gather he means to march on the jail and take Lenniger out, whether you try to stop them or not.'

Haggerty clamped his teeth tight, hitched up the gunbelt around his middle. 'Thanks for the warnin', Miss Julie. I figured he might try somethin' like this but it could be serious. I'll just step along to the jail and be waitin' for him when he arrives.'

'Do you think there's going to be trouble? I know a few men who would help. They don't like what Dryden is trying to do.'

Haggerty shook his head. 'I don't want to split this town right down the middle and set one group at the throats of another. That way, we would be finished. But if I can hold them off for another hour or so, young Bob Travers might get back here with—'

He noticed her eyes widen just a shade and a curiously soft expression on her features. 'With Rick Hartnell.' She breathed the words.

'That's right.' He nodded. 'But I don't want you to go building up your hopes. By rights, if Travers had managed to locate him, they ought to have been here by sundown. He's my trump card. I figure that with him beside me, we can force the townsfolk to fall in with my plan and we'll have this town barricaded and shut up so tight that when those outlaws do decide to come, they'll be shot to pieces before they can get anywhere near the jail.'

'I hope you're right, Sheriff.' She paused for a moment, then turned her head as the murmur of voices from the other saloon carried loudly in the stillness.

Haggerty gave a brisk nod, then stepped off the broadwalk into the dusty street. 'I reckon it might be safer if you were to go home and stay there,' he warned. 'Put up the shutters if you like. I wouldn't like anyone to come along and take another shot through one of the windows.'

Her eyes clouded for a moment, then she walked quickly along the broadwalk without a backward glance, crossed the opening of one of the narrow alleys, and was lost to sight. Haggerty paused only for a moment, watching her retreating figure and then walked swiftly to the jailhouse, opened the door, locking and bolting it behind him. Moving across to the wall, he took down one of the rifles from the clips, loaded it, then placed it carefully against the wall just beside the door. There was no sound from the single occupied cell at the back of the building, but he felt certain that Lenniger was not asleep, that the outlaw had guessed at the mood of the townsfolk and would know what was happening just as well as anyone else in town.

CHAPTER SEVEN

Siege Town

The talking over at the saloon continued for the next hour or so. It meant that Dryden was probably succeeding in getting the men there really steamed up, Haggerty reflected, but it also meant that time was passing and every minute that slipped by without those men making some positive action, meant time on his side. He went to the window more frequently now, peered along the dark street in the direction of the desert trail to the east of town, but it remained empty. After a while, he too, began to doubt if Travers and Hartnell would ever come.

When the sharp knock came at the door, he jerked in his seat, then pulled one of the Colts from its holster and went over to the door.

'Who's there?' he called harshly.

'Matt Thompson.' The other's voice was muffled by the thick door, but still recognizable.

He unbolted the door and let the old man in, noticing the ancient rifle he carried in his hand. A quick glance along the street, a look at the yellow light that still spilled from the windows and over the doors of the saloon on the opposite side, then he stepped back into the office and slid the bolts back into place.

'You were a goddamned fool to come here, Matt,' he

said harshly. Tension gave an added edge to his tone. He thrust the Colt back into its holster, motioned the other to a chair. 'You were at death's door when I last saw you.'

'Reckon it'll take a lot more than that to kill an old coot like me, Sheriff,' he grunted. 'Besides, Julie mentioned that Dryden is trying to talk some of the men into attacking the jail and letting Lenniger go free. I don't aim to see that happen if I can help it. Reckon I can still shoot straight if they try anythin'.'

'Dryden will have a lot of men with him,' Haggerty said quietly. 'He's a slick and clever talker and I guess he's got a point.'

'You ain't sayin' he's in the right, wantin' to let this killer go free?' The older man's eyes had grown bright and hard, but with a feverish glitter in them and Haggerty noticed that whenever he moved, he pressed his lips tightly together, teeth biting into the lower one, as pain jarred through his chest. There was still a bandage wound tightly around him, restraining his movements.

Haggerty looked at him with a swift, sharpened interest. Then he glanced up quickly as the sound of voices in the distance suddenly swelled in volume. He heard loud shouts, then the sound of men spilling from the saloon, out into the street. Quickly, he reached out and grabbed the rifle from its place at the wall.

'Better get over by the window, old-timer,' he said harshly. 'This time, they sound as if they mean business.'

'Queer thing this, the ordinary, decent citizens of the town moving in against the Sheriff,' mused the other as he edged towards the wall, pressing himself close in beside the window.

'When they face up to big trouble like this, they forget that they're decent citizens,' muttered Haggerty, extinguishing the lamp and leaving the room in darkness. 'All that bothers them then is saving their own skins and they're ready and willin' to forsake anythin' for that.'

Adjusting his eyes quickly to the dark, he moved across

to the door. The sound of the approaching crowd grew outside. He could hear Dryden's high-pitched squeaky tone clashing stridently with the others. The crowd came along the street and then paused directly outside the Sheriff's Office.

'Reckon they're just tryin' to get up their courage to come on in,' grunted Thompson contemptuously.

'They won't take long,' nodded the Sheriff. 'More'n half of 'em will have the false courage that comes from too much whiskey. Dryden will have seen to that. He must be a very scared man to go through with this.'

'You inside, Sheriff?' Dryden's voice reached them from outside.

Moving forward, Haggerty shot back the bolts of the door, still holding the Winchester in his right hand. Thompson glanced round quickly. 'You ain't goin' out there to 'em, are you, Sheriff?'

'I've got to try to talk a little sense into 'em, Matt.' Pulling open the door, Haggerty stepped out on to the broadwalk, hefting the rifle into his hands. He cocked it ominously.

'You want somethin', Dryden?' he said thinly.

The other hesitated, did not seem to relish the position of leader of this mob which he had assumed. Then he stepped forward. 'That's right, Slim. Now don't make things worse for yourself. We want Lenniger and we mean to have him. Once he's turned loose, maybe we can get around to talking things over, get this town back into the old ways again.'

'Back into fear from these owlhoots, you mean.' snapped Haggerty thinly. He swung the rifle to cover the men as the crowd threatened to surge forward for the steps leading into the office. 'I intend to shoot the first man who tries to come in here,' he said ominously. There was no mistaking the seriousness in his voice. 'That goes for you too, Dryden. I don't know what's got into you men. You seem anxious enough to follow a banker when he suggests letting an out-and-out killer go free so that he can raid the territory and ride down into town whenever he feels like it, but you won't back me in my stand against these outlaws.'

'We know what we're doing, Sheriff,' called one on the men thickly. 'Your way will mean the end of the town. Our way means that there'll be no trouble.'

'Is that what Dryden has told you?' Haggerty's scornful tone lashed the men. 'Because if it is, then he's wrong. Do you think for one minute that Lenniger is going to spare this town, just because you let him go free. That's the sign of weakness that he's waitin' for. He knows then that you won't fight no matter what he does and the next time he comes ridin' in, he'll make his demands and you'll have no chance but to do exactly as he says. D'you want the gamblers and killers back again like in the old days? You fought hard enough to rid the town of them, fifteen years back.'

The men fell silent at that and he knew that he had them wondering. Only Dryden spoke up, edging forward a little. 'Don't listen to him, men. Sure we elected him, Sheriff. But I guess we can get him out of this post and put in somebody else who'll do as he's told.'

'Get away from here,' said Haggerty. 'You damned fool, Dryden – get away. I warned you that I'd shoot down Lenniger rather than see him go free. I mean that. Now call off these men you've brought with you, or by God I'll—'

One of the men shouted something in a harsh tone. He drew his gun and fired at the shattered window of the office. The bullet sent glass tinkling into the street. A second later, there was the sound of a rifle shot from inside and the man staggered back, clutching at his bleeding shoulder, the sixgun dropping from his hand into the dust.

'He's got somebody in there with him,' yelled Dryden. 'He ain't alone.'

'That's right.' Haggerty raised his voice to make himself heard above the confused yelling. The men began to retreat very slowly from the building. He could see that they were not finished yet. There was still some of the rebellious nature in them which was not broken, even by that shot from inside the building.

He heard Doc Thornton crying out somewhere in the middle of the mob and a moment later, the other had thrust his way forward, shouldering the others to one side. He came up to where Dryden stood a little apart from the others.

'You can't browbeat us, Haggerty. We know our rights.'

'Mebbe so, but letting prisoners free isn't one of 'em.' Haggerty lifted the rifle again as the other came forward purposely.

Thornton gave him a studying glance, and for a moment an answer seemed to be balanced in his mind, but before he could speak, another voice at the back of the crowd said: 'I reckon the Sheriff's got a point there, men. Better scatter and leave peaceful like. You'll get all of the fighting you want in a little while.'

Haggerty glanced up, recognizing the voice instantly, feeling the sense of relief that washed through his taut body and mind. It had been a measure of their concentration on the mob in front of the Office that no one had heard or noticed the two men ride up from the desert trail at the end of town, until they were seated only a few yards from the men.

'Rick Hartnell. Boy, am I glad to see you here. Figured you'd never get back.' Haggerty laid the rifle down beside the open door of the office and stepped down into the street, pushing his way through the throng of men who had turned to face the men behind them. He knew there would be no danger from this mob now. All of the fight had suddenly gone out of them. He saw Dryden whisper something to Doc Thornton and then the two men slipped away into the shadows. They had made their play, but the gamble had failed at the last moment.

Hartnell swung himself easily from the saddle, then nodded towards Travers.

'Reckon you'd better get a doctor to take a look at him, Sheriff. He ran into trouble on the other side of the desert. Four of those outlaws tried to crowd him just before I got there.'

'Sure, sure.' Haggerty helped the other from the saddle, peered anxiously at Travers's face. 'You did a damned good job, Bob. When I heard that there were some of those outlaws on your tail, I doubted if you'd make it.'

'Hell, I nearly didn't.' The other forced a quick grin then pressed his lips tightly together. 'What was that huckus about when we arrived?'

'Just Dryden trying to get the men to rush the jailhouse and free Lenniger. Nothing of importance now that you're here.'

'I figure they'll ride in before morning,' said Rick quietly. He watched the men scurry away, saw a crowd of them return to the saloon where the lights still shone yellow in the dimness, then turned and nodded towards the end of the street. 'And I reckon that's the way they'll come. They won't waste time and effort riding around to the north and coming in from the other end.'

'You've got a plan to stop 'em?' Haggerty looked at him closely, a flicker of hope showing in his eyes.

'We'll need help. Better go and pick out any men who'll help you. Then get some wood, wagons, anything to form a barricade across the street between here and the end of the street. In the meantime, you got any idea where we can get some gunpowder?'

'Gunpowder?' Haggerty shot him a quick glance. 'How much do you want?'

'A couple of barrels ought to be enough for my purpose. I figure that we have to throw 'em in confusion before they hit the main street, maybe finish half of them before they hit the town. If we do that, it ought to put a little backbone into some of the men here.'

'Downing, the gunsmith will have some gunpowder. Guess he can let you have a couple of barrels.'

'Good. Then you round up as many men as you can. Leave the rest to me.'

After the other had gone, moving over towards the saloon, he made his way along the street until he came to the gunsmith's shop. It was in darkness and he knew there was a strong possibility that the other was with those men back there in the saloon. Going up into the porch, he turned the bell briskly.

For several moments there was no sign of life in the house, then a light sprang into being upstairs and fifteen seconds later, he heard the sound of heavy footsteps clumping down the stairs, coming towards the door. A lock and chain rattled, then the door swung open and a man stood there, peering out, his greying hair rumpled. His eyes were narrowed from sudden awakening.

'Yes, who is it?'

'I've come from the Sheriff,' Rick said quickly, insistently. 'I need your help.'

'At this hour?' A pause, then the other stepped to one side. 'Oh well, come inside.'

Rick moved along a wall-papered passage and then into the parlour of the house. Downing stood blinking in the light of the lamp as he lit it and placed it on the table, then faced him. 'Now, mister,' he said thickly. 'What call have you for wakening me like this? What can I do for the Sheriff?'

'There's a big chance that those outlaws will come riding into town before morning,' Rick said, 'and if we want to stop 'em—'

The gunsmith pulled his brows down into a thick line and a look of puzzlement crossed his coarse features. 'But . . . but Dryden was going to have it out with the Sheriff, get Lenniger out of jail and run him out of town.'

'He changed his mind,' said Rick easily. 'We're going to shoot up those outlaws when they do come and for that, I need some gunpowder.'

Downing sat down abruptly, his gaze fixed on Rick's face. 'Gunpowder.'

'That's right. I need two barrels. If you want any authority, I reckon you'd better get dressed and we'll both go along and have a word with Haggerty. But there isn't any time to waste. He's out there now rounding up as many men as he can, and pretty soon they'll start barricading the town. By the time those killers ride into Hammer Bend, they're going to find a fighting force ranged against 'em.'

'You're joking. We can't hope to fight off those killers.'

'We're going to try. It's about time this town stood on its own two feet and faced up to things as they are, instead of how they'd like them to be.'

The look of bewilderment on the other's face cleared as he got to his feet. 'I know you now,' he said tightly. 'You're that gunslick, Hartnell, who came here a few days ago and led that posse who brought in Lenniger.'

'That right.' Rick made no attempt to deny it. He did not know what effect this would have on the other's inclination to help him.

Downing paused for a moment, then shrugged. 'I'll get you the powder,' he said softly. 'I thought, a while ago, that Dryden's plan was the best for everybody concerned, but now I'm not so sure. I figure we've given in to these killers for too long. We've got to dig in our heels somewhere along the line, or we're finished.'

He picked up the lamp and led the way out of the room, along a short passage to the rear of the house. Pushing open a door, he went inside, taking care to place the lamp on a wide, wooden ledge. Glancing about him, Rick realized why the other had done this. Against the far wall were several wooden casks and he knew that each would be filled to the brim with gunpowder. It required only one single spark and the whole place would go up around them.

'There it is,' said Downing. He pointed. 'Take what you need. 'I'll square things with the Sheriff tomorrow.' He grinned wryly. 'If we're still around then.'

'Two kegs will be enough for what I've got in mind.' He picked up one of the kegs, surprised at its weight.

Downing grabbed another. 'Guess I'd better come along with you if you've no objection. I'd like to do a little to stop these killers.'

'Better get yourself some clothes on,' Rick observed. 'It's cold out there.'

He waited in the small parlour while the other went back upstairs, returning a few moments later, fully dressed, carrying an ancient shotgun over his shoulder. Rick eyed the weapon coldly, then nodded to himself. When it came to a tight corner a gun like that was a better weapon than a rifle or a sixgun. There was something about a shotgun that could put a touch of fear into any man because although a slug could miss, or lodge in a non-vital part of the body, several ounces of lead could always be relied upon to find a vital spot.

He picked up the cask of gunpowder and led the way to the door, stepping out into the street. There were a few people in sight. From the saloon across the way, he could just make out the vague murmur of voices, guessed that Haggerty was doing his best to swing the people over to his side. But that was something he would have to leave to the Sheriff. There was plenty for him to do in the small amount of time they had available, even with Downing helping.

At the edge of town, where the trail led out over the narrow creek, and then into the desert before winding up into the hills, they paused while Rick studied the terrain which lay silent around them in the darkness. He grinned a little at the expression which the man's face beside him held. 'They're sure to come this way when they ride in. I reckon we've got to set the trap here.'

'You're going to bury the gunpowder here?'

'That's right. One keg on either side of the trail, among those rocks yonder. It ought to stop them for a little while and spook their mounts at least.'

'I figured you might need this fuse too.' The other dug into his jerkin and pulled out the reel of fuse which he laid across the bridle of his mount.

Rick cursed himself for not remembering that himself. He was glad now that the other had come along with him. But then, Downing was obviously a man who had handled gunpowder most of his life, knew every aspect of it.

'The success of this plan of yours is going to depend on a lot of things,' muttered Downing. He slid from his saddle and lifted down the keg of powder. Holding it under one arm, he stepped off the trail and stood waiting for Rick to join him.

'I realize that. What I'm wondering about is the effect of the blast when these go off.'

Downing pursed his lips. 'If those killers are within twenty feet of the powder when it goes they'll be killed outright,' said Downing positively.

'This looks to be the right spot.' He went over to the pile of rocks where they reared up over the trail, forming a kind of natural overhang. It took only a few moments for him to locate the narrow fissure set four feet from the edge which overlooked the trail. Downing looked down in satisfaction. 'It's not too deep,' he observed, 'so there's little change of muffling the blast, but it's deep enough to hide the keg.'

When they had finished there, with the length of fuse snaking from the hole punched in the top of the wooden keg, they moved over to the other side of the trail which narrowed a little at this point. Rick deliberately chose a point several yards beyond where they had set the other charge. If one charge failed to have its full effect, there was always the chance that the other might do some damage.

It was an old trick this, one they had used often during the war. A nasty way of fighting, but here the ends justified the means. It was only by using a trick such as this that he stood a chance of getting the townsfolk on to their side.

Downing straightened with a grunt, surveyed their handiwork. 'That ought to do it,' he muttered. 'I've judged the fuse as best I can. Give or take a few seconds, I reckon we can judge it pretty nicely.'

Rick climbed back in to the saddle, struck a match and shielded it with his hand, staring down at his watch. 'I'm sorry to have to ask you to do this, but I want to check with Haggerty on how things are going back in town. I need someone to stay here and keep a sharp lookout for those *hombres* if they decide to ride into town.'

'I'll do it.' The other gave a quick nod. 'You want me to light the fuse if they do head this way?'

'You know what to do? Don't make any mistake for God's sake. I don't want any innocent bunch of men blown to pieces.'

'Don't worry none on that score.' Downing rubbed the back of his hand across his mouth. 'I'll keep watch. I know how to handle this stuff.'

Rick wheeled his mount. 'I'll be as quick as I can. Once I'm sure the town is ready, I'll head back and join you.'

He gigged his mount, rode back into town. He noticed with satisfaction that the main street was no longer empty. A couple of wagons had been moved into position so that they lay across the width of the street and Haggerty was supervising the proceedings. He walked quickly over to Rick as he spotted the other, glanced up.

'You just come from the desert trail?'

'That's right. I left Downing there. We've mined the road just beyond the creek. I reckon if they come that way we can stop more than half of them. How are things going here?'

'Pretty well. I managed to talk most of 'em into helping

me. They still aren't too keen to tote guns against these killers. Can't blame 'em, I suppose. Haven't seen any sign of Dryden and Thornton since that ruckus outside the office. I suppose they're around somewhere, but we don't need them.'

'You seem to have made a pretty good barricade here. Any squeak out of Lenniger yet?'

'Ain't heard nothin'. I guess he's keepin' quiet, knows things are goin' against him.'

'Better keep an eye on him, stay close to the jail. I've an idea that Dryden may still try to pull somethin', even at this late hour. You hurt his pride back there when you faced him with the crowd. He won't forget that in a hurry and this is the only way at the moment he can get back at you.'

Haggerty's eyes held a curious expression. 'You reckon he'd do a thing like that, even now when the feeling of the townsfolk is against it?'

'No tellin' what a man will do when he's been made to look a fool in front of his friends.'

Haggerty gave a slow nod. 'You could be right, I suppose. I'll have a couple of men keep watch on the cells.'

'I'll be ridin' back to join Downing. Don't feel easy leaving him alone out there. He knows gunpowder, I guess, but he doesn't know these killers and he has only a shotgun to defend himself with.'

'Sure, Rick. I'll keep an eye on things here. Better yell when you come hightailin' it back into town. The men are likely to be trigger-happy and they may fire at anybody who comes ridin' in.'

'We'll be careful.' Turning, he rode along the wide street, the hooves of his mount lifting tiny spurts of dust. Behind him, he heard another wagon being pushed and manhandled into place. How many of these men would stand and fight when it came to the showdown, he wondered inwardly. He hoped for twenty, better still forty.

But he might be lucky if he got a dozen men to stand their ground when the lead started flying in earnest. Even that might be enough if his plan worked.

He found Downing crouched among the rocks, with his mount tethered a few yards away. He scrambled down from his vantage point.

'Seen anythin'?'

'Nope. But I figure they'll still come. It'll be dawn within a few hours and it ain't like these criters to attack in broad daylight. They usually like everythin' on their side.'

'I agree. But I wish they'd hurry. It's this waiting that's goin' to get on everybody's nerves.'

'I feel the same way.' The other shivered in the cold night air. 'I only hope to God this plan of yours works. If it doesn't we're finished.'

'You got everything ready?'

'All set. It's going to be a touchy thing. Seconds are going to make all the difference here.'

They remained silent for long moments after that, each man engrossed in his own thoughts. Too much was at stake for Rick to feel quite as confident as he had when he had ridden into the street of Hammer Bend a couple of hours earlier.

When he heard the run of a horse coming from the direction of town, he jerked upright, stared off into the darkness. Beside him, Downing came to his feet, held the shotgun tightly in his hands.

'Hold your fire,' Rick whispered tautly. 'They're coming from town.'

He moved over to the edge of the trail, listened to the horse come on, moving fast. Caution and interest rose in him together. Sound and rider came together around the bend in the road, then over the bridge across the creek. He heard the thin squeal of reins as the rider pulled sharply on the bit, saw the dark shape in the saddle straighten back. Then the horse inched forward and he knew that the rider was searching about for some sign of them.

He stepped out into the middle of the trail, then paused in sudden surprise as a woman's familiar voice came to him out of the darkness. 'That you, Rick?'

'Julie!' He moved forward, reached for the reins, holding them tightly in his hand. 'What are you doing here? Don't you know there's going to be trouble here soon?'

'I know. That's why I came.'

Downing moved forward, out of the shadow of the boulders overlooking the narrow trail. 'You'd better turn around and ride on back into town, Miss Julie,' he said harshly. 'These critters will be riding this trail any minute now if they're comin' at all. We don't want you to get mixed up in it. This is goin' to be man's work.'

In answer, the girl slid easily from the saddle, landed lightly on the hard, rocky ground, pulling the rifle from its scabbard as she did so. 'I think I can handle a rifle as well as you can, Mr Downing,' she said defiantly. 'And it's pretty obvious they don't need me back in town.'

'Downing is right, Julie,' said Rick tightly. 'When those men come riding this way, we have to move real fast. Once these fuses are lit, nothing's going to stop the gunpowder from blowing. But every second is going to count and we can't afford to leave anythin' to chance.'

'I'm staying.' There was a note of determination in her voice that brooked no refusal.

Rick shrugged his shoulders. 'All right. But be careful and do exactly as I say. We won't have too much warning when they come.'

The girl touched his arm in reply, nodded her head and even in the dimness he could see the long brown hair lying on her shoulders and the lovely turn of her throat. She still seemed to guard against him, but he could not tell why that might be. For a moment she stood close to him and he could feel the warmth of her. Then she moved away to one side, among the rocks edging on to the trail, the rifle gripped tightly in her hands.

Rick turned to the man beside him. 'I think I'd as soon

trust her with us as any of the men back in town,' he said quietly.

The other's smile was a white thing in the shadow of his face. 'She's too willful and headstrong,' he said, eyes narrowed a little on Rick in sudden appraisal. 'Known her since she was a baby. Just like her mother. Always determined to have her own way. She's going to need a lot of taming, I'm thinking.'

Rick nodded, then lifted his head a little, straining his ears to pick out the tiny sounds of the night. The moon was just beginning to show low in the east where its light touched the clouds there with a pale yellow glow that was brightening with every second that passed. Except for the slight jingle of bridle metal from the horses a few yards away and the sighing click of the wind in the sparse mesquite on top of the rocky stretch of ground nearby, the night was silent and a churchly stillness lay over everything.

Reaching into his pocket, he pulled out his tobacco pouch and built himself a smoke, then handed the pouch to Downing. They smoked in silence as they waited but each minute was a growing weight on them. When he had first heard of the trouble in this territory he had felt a certain inward haste, a sense of urgency that would not be denied, but the past week or so had brought a patience in him that was such that time now did not seem to matter very much.

Turning his head, he glanced in the direction of the girl, saw that she had seated herself on one of the smooth outcrops of rock and was staring thoughtfully into the distance in the direction of the sky-rearing mountains, their peaks now touched with the first yellow rays of the rising moon. The trees on the higher slopes trapped the shadowy pearl light long before the moonlight came creeping over the low valley and touched the trail.

'Somebody comin'.' There was a sharp note to Downing's voice as he turned suddenly, head cocked a little on one side.

Rick listened in silence for several moments, before he picked out the heavy sound of horses moving downgrade from the distant hills. In the clear, cold air sound carried far and well and he guessed these riders were the best part of ten miles distant. Glancing at the man beside him, he saw the change of his lips and the small gust of expression that passed over his features, the way he moved a little towards the rocks, tossing the cigarette on to the ground and grinding it out with the heel of his boot.

'Don't reckon there's any doubt about it.' There was a sharp edge to his voice. 'You all set to light those fuses?'

'Ready whenever you give the word,' acknowledged the other.

Aided by the bright moonlight, it was possible to pick out the tightly-bunched group of men as they swung out of the tree-lined slopes and headed across the plain. Too far for him to be able to make any accurate guess as to their numbers, he knew that there were far more there than had ridden with Lenniger when the band had been smashed. Doubtless they had been reinforced by men brought in from the south and east. There were always bands of men ready to join up with these ruthless killers, anxious to share the spoils whenever a town was attacked or a stage coach held up and robbed. Some would join just for the sheer brutal joy of killing, of thumbing their noses at the law they despised.

No doubt the outlaws had promised these men easy picking, promised them a town that was wide open, and once Lenniger was released from jail, they could continue with their plundering and killing.

For a moment, Rick felt the white-hot anger seething within him, forced a quick control of his emotions and temper. This was the time for quick thinking and ice-cool nerves. He only hoped that Downing knew as much about those fuses and that powder as he claimed he did. One wrong move, one mistake, and the three of them could be blown to Kingdom Come and then the town would really be wide open for these outlaws.

He threw a swiftly apprehensive glance in Downing's direction, but the other had walked coolly towards the rocks where one of the fuses snaked down between the tall pinnacles. He had the box of sulphur matches in his hand, ready for when the time came. The girl had risen to her feet once she had heard the thunder of the approaching riders. Now she moved down from the boulders and stood close beside him.

'Once you've lit the charges, what do you intend to do?' she asked in a low voice.

'If we're lucky, the gunpowder should put at least half of them out of action. We'll head back to town, wait for the others there, if they still have enough nerve to come.'

She looked at him with a moment's penetrating attention. Then she asked: 'Do you think they'll ride into town if you do succeed in killing half of them?'

'Who knows? Without Lenniger they're finished in this territory. I reckon most of 'em know that.'

'So you reckon they'll still ride into town?'

He nodded slowly. 'We've got to be ready for them. Even half of those killers could give us the fight of our lives.'

The cold moonlight lay over the rocks, touching the deep gullies with midnight strokes of blackness. Another mile and he could make out the individual riders as they converged on the trail, pushing their mounts at a cruel pace.

'Looks as if they're in a mighty big hurry to get into town,' grunted Downing. He bent and held the end of the fuse in one hand, his head lifted so that he might watch the approaching men. They waited. For a time, Rick kept his eyes on the men as they spurred their mounts over the moon-washed plain. He could feel the tightness beginning to grow within him once more, knew that this time, it would be difficult for him to control it completely. The thunder of hoofs was sharper now and more insistent.

Rick ran his tongue over his lips. He could feel the girl trembling a little beside him, could make out the white-knuckled grip of her hands on the rifle, knew that she was holding herself in with a tremendous effort.

'How soon?' asked the gunsmith, glancing round.

'Soon enough,' said Rick quietly. He looked towards the riders, saw that they were now beginning their wide swing that would bring them out of the narrow strip of bare desert and on to the trail perhaps a mile away. 'We've got to be sure this time. You're sure you've timed that fuse right?'

'Everythin' is as close as we can get it,' the other assured him.

'Then be ready when I give the word. Once that fuse is runnin', head back for the horses and saddle up. You understand?'

Downing and the girl nodded. Still Rick waited, a look of stony patience on his face, his features so still that they might have been carved from granite. Five minutes. Ten. Then the riders were moving in swiftly. He heard a hard, hoarse laugh, someone yell a sudden order. They had ridden down out of the hills and were on their way to Hammer Bend, a town that waited in fear for their coming, a town where there were no men with the courage to lift a gun and face up to them, where the men would cower inside their houses rather than venture out on to the street and back their Sheriff in his attempt to keep law and order. A few more minutes; another half mile, and they would be running wild through the streets of the town. Or so they thought . . .

Their confidence, thought Rick inwardly, would have made them careless. Had they not been so sure of themselves, had they paused to consider the possibility that things might not go exactly as they planned, they might have foreseen the possibility of a trap somewhere along the trail into town. As it was, they came towards the narrow gap in the trail just before it crossed the creek at a quick gallop, scarcely pausing to slow their pace.

'Now?' muttered Downing. He held the box of matches in his fist.

'Not yet . . .' said Rick. He was watching the men as they approached, trying to judge their speed, to relate it to the burning speed of that length of fuse.

'Now.'

The order was barely more than a husky whisper, but Downing moved quickly, instinctively. The flare of the match was hidden from anyone on the trail by the rocks. There was a faint spit from the end of the fuse as it began burning. Then Downing had run, doubled over, across the trail, to where the other fuse lay on the rocks. Another brief orange flare, then that too had been lit.

'Let's go,' Rick said thickly. He turned and made for the horses, the girl and the gunsmith close on his heels. Swiftly, he swung himself up into the saddle, threw a quick glance behind him. They had not been seen. The trail wound a little before it came in under the wide overhang.

The girl was mounted, moving off before he gigged his own horse forward. Downing rode alongside him, features tight. The same thought was uppermost in all of their minds at that moment. Had they timed things right? Would the fuse continue to burn throughout the whole of its length. Explosives were such strange and unpredictable things. Handled correctly by someone who had spent his life with them, they performed reasonably satisfactorily. But even then, there was always that chance that something could go wrong. It was a chance that no man could really guard against.

In his mind's eyes, he could visualize that tiny red spark travelling along that winding, twisting length of fuse, drawing ever closer to those two kegs of sleeping hell. It needed only the slightest spark there and those two barrels would blow and if they had done things well, the explosions would take half of those killers down to hell before they knew what was happening.

They crossed the creek where it shone yellow in the moonlight, rode up the incline on the other side. Behind them, they could hear the strident abrasion of hoofs on the hard, stony ground, knew that the outlaws were gaining on them with every second, that their lives now depended on Downing's knowledge and handiwork.

Every second that passed now seemed like an eternity. There were so many things which could have gone wrong, thought Rick tightly, so many imponderables which they may not have taken into account. A hundred possibilities went through his mind, were considered, and then rejected instantly as the night erupted behind them, the deep-throated explosions sounding almost together.

CHAPTER EIGHT

Showdown

Turning instinctively in the saddle, reining his mount a little, Rick glanced back over his shoulder. The dull red flashes of the explosions rivalled even the brilliant yellow of the moonlight, but it was not this which immediately attracted his attention; it was the stupendous sight of hundreds of tons of rock being lifted high into the air, held there for what seemed an eternity by the titanic force of the explosive, then hurled down on the bunch of riders as they passed between the two charges. Several of the riders were blown from their saddles by the tremendous power of the blast and he saw horses go down as the rocks fell on them from all sides.

Even from that distance, he felt the sudden surge of the blast wave against his body, reeling him a little in the saddle and the scream of the horses and the injured men sounded above the dying, rumbling echoes which roared away over the plains. Glancing quickly back, he saw that the girl had squeezed her eyes tightly shut as if to blot out the image of the scene. Dirt and bits of rock began to shower down about them as well as the trapped men, obscuring them from Rick's eyes. Dust went down into his throat with every breath he drew into his lungs.

Choking a little, he wheeled his mount, yelled at the

others loudly, raising his voice to make himself heard above the din. 'Start riding – back to town.'

Behind them, the terrified horses, those still on their feet, were milling around aimlessly where the trail had vanished, been obliterated under the mass of rock. They could make out the sounds of their plunging hoofs, the angry cursing of the men still in the saddle as they fought to control their bucking mounts, fought to move them out of the cloud of choking dust that still hung in the air.

A few of the horses had bolted across the plains, bucking and leaping. Others were being fought to a halt. It would not be long before the outlaws who were still alive, still in a condition to ride into town, regained their wits and came after them. They headed quickly back into town, rode down the main street towards the barricade that had been hastily erected across the middle of the street. Sliding from the saddle, Rick helped Julie Thompson down, then slapped his sorrel hard on the rump, sending it galloping off into the shadows. He moved quickly around to the rear of the wagons, found Haggerty there with perhaps a score of men. Some carried rifles, others had sixguns in their hands. They all looked quiet and determined men, ready to fight, but how long would their courage last when the testing time came?

'We heard the explosions,' grunted Haggerty thinly. He straightened up. 'How'd it go?'

'I figure we may have stopped half of 'em. But don't build up your hopes too much on that score. They've been joined by more men, other killers like themselves. Probably they've brought in men from down south, ready for an easy picking at a town like this. Word must've got around that we don't intend to fight when they come. I think that trap on the trail yonder may have changed their minds a little on that point.'

'You sure about these other men ridin' with 'em?'

'No mistake about it.' Rick pulled out the Colts, checked them carefully, then thrust them back into their holsters. 'I reckon we've got five minutes at the most before they hit town. Everybody know what to do?'

'I guess so.' Haggerty forced a quick nod. 'I've got a couple of men keeping an eye on the jailhouse yonder, just in case Dryden and Thornton do try somethin'. I reckon myself they've hidden themselves away someplace until this blows over.'

'We can do without men like that.' Rick settled himself behind the wheel of one of the wagons, peered through the radiating wooden spokes along the silent length of the street where it stretched away in darkness until it met the desert trail. He pulled in a deep breath of the cool night air, felt a little sweat on his forehead. He hoped that the men there would hold their fire until he gave the word. He wanted to empty as many saddles as possible with their first volley, before the outlaws could dismount and get under cover. If any man fired out of turn it could ruin their plan.

As he waited there in the tense, clinging silence, he tried not to think of what might happen to the town if they failed that night. They would never get a second chance to destroy these outlaws, these ruthless killers, and Dryden would get his way, set Lenniger free if the outlaws didn't do it themselves before taking over the town. But that was something in the future and he tried to put the idea out of his mind. Such thoughts only served to slow a man's reflexes to danger point when the time came for quick and instant action. He moistened his lips and glanced about him at the rest of the men, their features just visible in the flooding moonlight that washed along the street, sober-faced men who knew what they were up against and were still not sure whether they stood a chance at all of succeeding.

'Why in God's name don't they come?' grunted one of the men close by.

'They'll be here in their own good time,' Rick answered, raising his voice a little so that most of the men could hear. 'Those explosions will have warned them that they can't take us by surprise, that we're ready and waiting for 'em.'

How many men were still alive out there? he wondered tensely. It was just possible that they had decided against riding into town, that they were playing it clever, had ridden back into the hills and would return when they were least expected. He smiled a little grimly to himself in the dimness. The ground under his body was hard and dust kept working its way into his nostrils. He doubted if the outlaws would do that. They had to get Lenniger out of jail and the longer they put that off, the stronger would Haggerty's hand be in town, and time would pass quickly, bringing the circuit judge to Hammer Bend.

It was just possible that the outlaws were having second thoughts out there and they had decided against a frontal attack, had sent their men out on a wide detour around town, ready to fall on their rear without warning. Most of those men would have fought during the war, would know the advantage of taking your enemy from two sides.

Seconds ticked away and the silence that lay over the town now seemed to possess a strangely electric quality. Eyes were on the end of the street, peering into the flooding moonlight, straining to pick out the slightest movement there.

Rick's muscles tightened. He shifted his weight a little as cramp threatened to twist his legs into knots and his eyes narrowed, took on a hard and savage gleam. How much time had passed since those two twin explosions out there on the trail, since they had ridden from that scene of violence back into town? It seemed like an eternity, but could only have been twenty minutes, perhaps thirty.

'Here they come!' The warning was a vague shout from the other side of the street. Rick lifted his head. There, at the far end of the street, he just made out the riders as they entered the town and rode their horses at a walk along the street.

'Hold your fire until I give the word,' called Rick. 'Then make every shot count.'

He caught a fragmentary glimpse of one of the men lifting his rifle to his shoulder and sighting it on the men who rode towards the barricade. He knew from the thin, tight look on the man's face that he was sufficiently scared to pull that trigger before the outlaws were within killing range.

'Hold it, I said! Put that rifle down, you damned fool, if you can't do as you're told.'

Reluctantly, the man hesitated, then lowered the rifle, turned his head to glower at Rick. 'You intend to let 'em start breathing down on us before you shoot it out with 'em?' he said viciously, released tension sending a wave of anger through his body.

'Just be ready to fire when I give the word,' snapped Rick. 'The same goes for everybody.'

He narrowed his eyes, stared inflexibly at the advancing horsemen. The outlaws moved forward slowly, and even at that distance, he could see that some of them had been injured by the blast along the trail. They swayed in their saddles, but so long as they could handle a gun, they would be dangerous. He estimated there were twenty men in the bunch.

'Why haven't they opened fire yet?' muttered Haggerty. He moved his body a little, lying flat on the ground, the rifle held rigidly in his hands.

'They're probably hoping to scare us out into the open.' Rick thumbed back the hammers of the twin Colts. 'They don't want to rush us. We're in a strong position here, but if they can break the nerve of the men with us, they have a good chance of smashing our resistance.'

The men crouched low behind the shelter of the wagons, eyes bright as they watched the approach of the riders and wondered when the man at the end of the line would give them the order to fire. He seemed to be taking his time about it. What in God's name was he waiting for?

The same thought must have lived in the minds of all of the men at that moment as they watched the outlaws ride to within twenty yards of the barricade and still Hartnell had given them no sign. A few more yards and they could be right on top of them, breathing down their necks.

'Now?' asked Haggerty. He seemed as touchy as the others, lacked the deep patience that was in the younger man.

'Give them another few yards and we can empty nearly every saddle,' said Rick sharply. He was watching the men as they began to swing their mounts a little to either side so that they were no longer bunched so tightly, presenting so good a target for the guns of the men behind the barricade. 'Not yet,' said Rick thinly. He swung his head sharply. But the warning came a second too late. Over-anxious and certainly prompted by fear, one of the men had lifted his sixgun and squeezed the trigger. The sharp crash of the shot echoed along the street. One of the outlaws suddenly pitched sideways from his saddle. For a moment, his boot caught in the stirrup, then he slid to the street as his mount reared at the sudden shot, feet plunging into the yielding flesh of its rider.

But before the echoes of the shot had died away, the men were swinging from their saddles, dropping to the ground and working their way behind their mounts, moving towards the boardwalks, crouching out of sight. There was no point now in holding their fire. Rick began to pick off the running men as they tried to make it to cover. Shots sounded in a ragged and uneven rhythm from along the whole length of the barricade, lances of flame spearing stilleto-like into the darkness. One of the outlaws spurred his mount forward, body crouched low in the saddle, over the neck of his mount, legs clinging tightly to the horse's flanks as he fired at the defenders. Rick heard one of the men close beside him shriek a sudden warning as he saw the danger which raced towards them. Then the other had scrambled to his feet, had turned on his heel and was running back along the street, feet pounding in the dust.

Rick opened his mouth to yell a harsh warning, then closed it quickly, knew that it would come too late for the other. The outlaw's guns roared again and the running man threw up his arms and pitched forward on to his face in the dust, lying still in the middle of the street.

Rick had seen the danger coming. Already, the guns in his hands were lifted, barrels lined on the man as he rode down on them. Deliberately, Rick stayed his shots until the other was less than ten feet from the barricade, then squeezed the triggers, felt the guns buck against his wrists and knew that he had made no mistake.

He felt a bullet fan his cheek and another ploughed along the skin of his forearm, but in that same moment, his bullets caught the man in the throat and blood instantly soaked the front of the other's shirt. He stayed upright in the saddle briefly, then began to choke as he put both hands to his throat, fingers releasing their hold on the guns as if they were too heavy for him. Still coughing, he toppled sideways. The horse slithered to a halt directly in front of the barricade, then shied away.

Already, firing had broken out from behind the rails that bordered the sidewalks on both sides of the street, fire that poured into the barricade, seeking any weak points where the leaden slugs might penetrate the wooden barrier and find soft flesh and bone. A man, three feet from Rick, suddenly gave a mighty yell and flopped loosely forward, his hat falling to one side, exposing the wound in his neck. An outlaw screamed. A second, caught by a slug while he was in mid-stride, spun round on his heels like a marionette for several seconds before he fell in a crumpled, twisted heap.

'They're too well hidden now,' shouted Haggerty. He loosed off a couple of shots, then dropped the rifle and grabbed for his Colts.

'That goddamned fool who had to open fire before I

gave the word,' snapped Rick. Even as he spoke, his eyes had swung, were on the man who had somehow clambered along one of the wooden balconies around the upper storey of one of the nearby houses. Although the other was now crouched low, Rick could still just see him, knew that the other would be forced to lift himself if he wanted to fire a killing shot from that angle, and waited for the man to make his play. Lead struck the wheel in front of him, glanced off the metal rim with a shrill, high-pitched whine that shrieked in his ears. But he did not take his gaze from the other man.

Two seconds later, the outlaw made his move. Rick saw his head and shoulders lift slowly, eased themselves above the low rail that ran around the edge of the balcony. Gently, he lifted his gun, lined it up slowly, then fired.

For an instant, he thought that his shot had missed, that the bullet had gone wild. Then he saw that the other was no longer standing on his feet but lay draped against the rail, his body leaning forward, all of his body leaning forward, all of his inert weight thrown on the ancient, rotting wood. The rail snapped almost at once and the man pitched down into the street, his body turning over once before it hit the ground.

The gunfire increased in intensity. Now it was a terrible thing that lashed at them from three directions. There were still two or three of the outlaws in the middle of the street, lying on the ground behind the milling horses. Theirs was a precarious position. Although they were hidden from the return fire of the men behind the barricade, once the horses stopped their aimless milling and plunging and began to run, those men would stand no chance at all, they would all be trampled underfoot, trodden into red and bloody tatters of flesh and clothing.

A quick glance to his right and left and he noticed that their own casualties were relatively light at the moment. Two men killed and possibly three wounded. A small price to pay for the casualties they had already inflicted on the outlaws. He tried to see Julie Thompson, but there was no sign of the girl and he guessed she had slipped away during the earlier part of the fighting. He felt a little easier with that knowledge in his mind. This was no place for a woman even if she could handle a rifle as well as a man.

He lay flat now, sighting swiftly on the fleeting shadows that appeared at intervals behind the rails and rain-butts on the sides of the street. A small handful of the outlaws had managed to work their way into one of the empty buildings and were firing from the shelter of one of the downstairs rooms.

Every muscle in his body was so tight that it began to ache and the muscles along the front of his legs were corded with cramp, although his mind was very clear and sharp, taking in every sound and somehow magnifying it so that he was able to follow the trend of the firing, to guess where the main bunch of the enemy were.

He was not aware of the sudden movement behind him, until a man dropped down beside him in the dust and said hoarsely: 'Lenniger's free, Hartnell. That snake Dryden managed to get in to him ten minutes ago and let him out. He's running around loose somewhere and—'

Swiftly, angrily, Rick swung to his feet. There was the thin hum of a slug that struck the air close to his head as it fled by him, but he ignored it. 'How in God's name did that happen? I thought you had a couple of men watching the jail, Haggerty?'

'I did.' The other swung round sharply. 'Reckon they must've been taken by surprise.'

Rick gritted his teeth, felt the seething anger in him. He paused for a moment with his shoulders against one of the wooden uprights, then thrust fresh shells into the guns. His face was grim. 'I'm goin' after him,' he said thinly. 'He can't have got far but if he joins up with those men yonder, they'll ride back out of town and we won't have the chance to finish them.'

'He won't go to them right away.' The man who had thrown himself down beside him spoke urgently. 'He's – he's got Julie Thompson with him.'

For a moment, Rick could scarcely believe his ears. Then he grabbed the man by the shirt and hauled him roughly to his feet. 'Are you sure of this?'

Gulping, the man nodded. 'He's going to hold her hostage until you stop this shooting. Then he'll use her to make sure he can take over the town.'

Savagely, unable to control his anger, Rick hurled the other from him, did not even pause to glance down at him as the man sprawled on the dirt. Ducking his head, he ran across the street, up on to the broadwalk and quickly along it until he reached the Sheriff's Office. He couldn't afford to hesitate now. He had to move fast and hope that his instincts played him right. Worry stabbed at his mind, nagging him, giving him no rest. What did a man do now? Go after Lenniger and trust to God that he found the other before he had a chance to harm the girl? Even then, at that moment, he knew what the odds against that were, but surely there had to be a way. If it hadn't been for that accursed banker, that traitor who had let this hardened killer go, this would never have happened.

Maybe Dryden had never guessed that the other would do such a thing as kidnapping the girl; but that was no excuse. He hoped that he did not find the banker first, for he knew that he would surely kill the other if he did.

Swiftly, he stepped inside the outer office, stared about him. There was a lamp still burning low on the desk, but the room was empty. He saw signs of a struggle, a small chair had been overturned near the door leading out into the rear passage. Scowling he went through, back to the cells. The door of the one which had housed Lenniger was open and a dark shape lay across the entrance. He went down on one knee, turned the man over, knew in that moment that he would not have the satisfaction of evening the score with Dryden. The banker's dead face stared up at him, the eyes wide and unseeing, looking at something far beyond him.

His searching hand found the bullet wound in the other's chest. It had not bled a lot, but he knew that it would have proved instantly fatal. For a moment, there was a feeling of grim amusement in him. He could visualise what had happened. Instead of being grateful to his deliverer, Lenniger had shot down the man who had freed him, knowing that Dryden would be of no further use to him, that the other might talk.

Going all the way along the passage, he reached the rear door. It was open and he stepped through, into the narrow alley that linked with the main street in one direction and a twisting alley in the other. He reached his decision quickly. Lenniger would not have gone towards the main street. The heavy sound of firing came from that direction. No – he would have taken his captive in the other direction, was probably holed up in one of the deserted, abandoned houses at that very moment, crouched down behind one of the windows overlooking the alley, waiting for him to appear.

He pressed his body tightly in to the wall and began to ease himself along it, keeping to the shadows. His nerves were jumping irritably and he kept reviewing his decision to move in this direction, searching for flaws in it, but he could find none. Under the circumstances, this was the only course he could take. Lenniger would have guessed by now that once he discovered what had happened he would come after him; and that would suit the outlaw leader. He wanted Rick dead if he was to secure a place for himself in this territory. He knew, as well as anyone, that without him, these people would never stand up to tyranny.

Slowly, he moved forward, one hand trailing along the wall, feeling its roughness under his fingers, the other gripping the Colt, ready to use it at a moment's notice. He sensed the presence of Lenniger close by, although he could neither see him nor hear him.

The smell of the abandoned places came to him as he inched forward, trying to push his sight ahead of him. Here, in this narrow alley, the moonlight never succeeded in penetrating. It seemed to live in the eternal gloom of night. A rat scurried across the ground in front of him and he stopped quite still for several moments, not moving, every sense strained to pick out the location of Lenniger and the girl.

A moment later, he thought he heard a faint, muffled sound. Swiftly, he swung around, trying to trace the origin of the sound. It had been as if someone had tried to cry out, but the sound had been muffled by a hand roughly clapped over their mouth. He let his weight fall easy and slow now. In front of him there was the dull-grey square of a door with windows flanking it on either side, looking out on to the alley. He felt pretty certain that the sound had come from inside that house.

Another three paces forward and his outstretched hands touched the peeling paint on the wood of the door. Very gently, he pushed it open. It swung inward with a faint sigh of sound. For a long moment he stood there, motionless, trying to pin his mind on to what was happening, hoping to picture in his mind's eye the room that lay beyond the door, knowing that if Lenniger was there, he might have only a split second in which to act and fire if he was to stay alive and the girl was to remain unharmed. He did not doubt that the outlaw leader would gun her down if he had to. The other cared nothing for human life.

One step forward and a voice reached him from the darkness. 'I figured you'd come after me, Hartnell. I took the precaution of making sure that you didn't cause me any trouble.'

He tried to see the other before he spoke, but in the pitch blackness inside the room it was impossible, although he knew that the other was somewhere near the top of the flight of stairs which must have been on the far side of the room, for the outlaw's voice had come from the darkness in that direction.

Moistening his lips, he said tightly: 'If you've harmed the girl in any way, I'll—'

A mocking laugh cut through the room, choking him off. 'You'll what, Hartnell? Kill me? Maybe you're faster and more deadly with a gun than I am. I ain't denyin' that, but like you say, I've got the girl and that gives me the whip hand. This gun is against the back of her neck and believe me, I'll kill her if I have to.'

'Why don't you face up to the facts, Lenniger?' Rick kept himself behind the door as he spoke, 'You'll never get out of this town alive – and you know it. Your men are being cut to ribbons right now on the main street. We killed more'n half of 'em with gunpowder on the trail outside of town.'

'You think that's going to stop me getting out?' There was an unmistakable sneer in the other's tone. 'If you do, then you're wrong. With the girl, I can ride out any time I like. But first I've got a big score to settle with you, Hartnell and I'm a man who likes to pay his debts. I'm not going to be around when that circuit judge gets into Hammer Bend and it won't worry you because by then, you'll be under the earth on Boot Hill.'

'I'm coming after you,' said Rick flatly. He raised his voice a little. 'You all right, Julie?' He heard a faint movement at the top of the stairs, heard Lenniger mutter something hoarsely under his breath, then the girl said in a muffled whisper. 'I'm all right, Rick. He's got a gun like he says. But don't take any notice of his threats. Just come up and—' Her voice was cut off in mid-sentence and he guessed the other had clapped his hand over her mouth again, stopping the flow of words.

Anger roared through Rick's brain. For a moment he felt on the point of rushing headlong up the stairs, blundering forward in the darkness, oblivous of anything but the desperate, fierce desire to get his hands around the other's throat and squeeze the life from his body. With a tremendous effort, he fought to control himself. Anger was no good, blind rage could only destroy him.

'All right, Lenniger,' he hissed. He ducked his head the moment he spoke, then flung himself sharply to one side, kicking the door shut behind him with his foot. A gun flared in the darkness, the muzzle flash blooming crimson, the sound a shattering echo in the confined space. The bullet struck the door where Rick had been standing a split second earlier.

'Too bad,' muttered Rick, moving again, 'You wasted that one. I wasn't there.'

'I won't miss with the next one,' said Lenniger.

Rick listened carefully to the voice. He placed its source somewhere along the far side of the room and perhaps halfway up the stairs there or on a low balcony. He stopped, listening for the sound of the other, but heard nothing more. As he waited, he remembered those men who had been killed by Lenniger and his men, and not only by these outlaws, but by others. He remembered his mother and sister, shot down by men such as these and he turned suddenly cold and the hatred came washing through him again as it had so often before. Softly, walking on the balls of his feet, he worked his way around the room, keeping one hand touching the wall. He soon discovered the posts at the bottom of the stairs, ran his fingers over them slowly, peering up into the blackness above him. It seemed incredible that Lenniger and the girl could be standing motionless within five feet of him, but neither party could see the other.

Outside, he could hear the gunfire from the main street. It had not diminished at all during the past ten minutes. He guessed it was going to be more difficult to finish those outlaws than he had thought at the beginning. He only hoped that the men with Haggerty would stick it out and see this thing through. If they once threw in their hand, the town would be wide open and everything might be lost.

'You still there, Hartnell?' The voice came from almost directly above Rick. He swung, crouching low, remained silent. This was going to be a battle of nerves and the man who broke first would die. The silence grew. Vaguely he heard a movement at the dark top of the stairs. A muffled curse from Lenniger and then a dull, sickening thud that was distinctly audible. It was followed by the sound of a body falling against the floor and he knew what had happened even though he had been able to see nothing.

The girl had tried to struggle, might have thrown Lenniger off balance if she had persisted; so he had knocked her out with the heel of his gun. Maybe he had also thought that once Rick realized what had happened, he would make a move and give himself away. Tightening his lips, he moved closer to the bottom of the stairs, felt them with his fingers for a moment. There was dust there, thick and powdery. Crouching down low, he said: 'That was your last mistake, Lenniger. I'm coming forward now.'

A moment later, a bullet's explosion battered the silence of the room and the echoes chased each other from wall to wall, ringing in Rick's ears. The hot breath of the slug touched him. Then it ploughed into the floorboards close to his feet.

Deliberately, he let the silence build up. He guessed that the other had less pure nerve than most of the men he led; and Lenniger knew now that he could no longer use the unconscious girl as a shield. He had lost his chance of that when he had slugged her. A scrape of boots on the floor at the top of the stairs. Lenniger had realized the predicament he was in and was trying to back away, along the passage there and perhaps out of some window to the rear of the building.

Putting one foot on the lowest step of the stairs, Rick tested it with his weight. It did not creak as he had expected and he edged his way up the stairs one step at a time, holding his breath until it hurt in his lungs and the blood pounded behind his temples.

He heard Lenniger move again, a soft scrape of cloth against the wall. His hands touched the level ground of the upper floor, then he recoiled slightly, instinctively, as his fingers touched something warm and yielding. Julie! In the distance, he heard the man breathing, harsh, rasping sound which the other was unable to suppress. Carefully, he lifted himself to his feet, stepped over the girl's unconscious body. Now that his eyes were becoming accustomed to the pitch blackness here, he was able to make out details around him vaguely. In front of him, the passage stretched away for perhaps twenty feet and he imagined he saw the darker shape that was the outlaw less than ten feet away, body pressed tight against the wall.

Bringing up his gun, he fired, then threw himself to one side. The burned powder dazzled him momentarily; then muzzle light flared back at him and he realized that he had been tricked. Lenniger had been in one of the doorways that led off the passage and not where he had suspected he had seen him. The bullet fanned his cheek, struck the wall near him and whined off into the darkness. There was a tinkle of glass a moment later and he guessed that the ricochet had gone through one of the downstairs windows.

Swinging, Rick fired instinctively, and the second floor of the building rocked and quivered with the explosions. He fired three times, heard the quick scramble as the other darted from the doorway and ran for the end of the passage. The first two bullets missed their target, struck the walls, but the third found its mark as Lenniger reached the end of the passage, half-turned with his body vaguely outlined against the brighter patch that was the rear window. For a moment, he remained poised there, striving to hold life in his body and bring up the gun in his right hand, trying to line it up with Rick's chest. Then it slipped from his nerveless fingers and clattered to the floor at his feet as the outlaw swayed and teetered drunkenly. Rick moved forward, holding his Colt on the other, but there was no need to fire another shot. The other swayed back and a split second later, his body crashed through the window. Lenniger was lying sprawled in the rubbish of the yard below, his arms outstretched, his legs twisted under him.

Holstering the gun, Rick turned and made his way back to the top of the stairs. The girl twisted and moaned softly as he came up to her. Bending, he lifted her gently in his arms and carried her down the stairs. At the bottom, he paused for a moment, stared about him into the blackness of the house where death had come a few moments before, then stepped out into the alley. In the distance, a few desultory shots still sounded from the main street, but he knew that the gunfight was almost over. The outlaws had made their gamble and lost. They had failed in their attempt to ride in and take the town to pieces because the ordinary men of Hammer Bend had stood up against them, had let them come so far, but no further.

The street was littered with the outlaw dead as he stepped into it, then moved behind the shelter of the overturned wagons. Matt Thompson pushed himself to his feet, came hurrying forward as he spotted Rick.

'My daughter,' he said hoarsely 'Julie?'

'She'll be all right,' said Rick. 'He just hit her on the head, then tried to kill me.'

'Where is he now?' The other ground the words out between his teeth.

'He's back there, but you don't have to hurry. He's dead.'

Rick saw the fractional slump of the other's shoulders as he relaxed. He nodded. 'We've almost finished them here too. Can't be many of 'em still alive.'

'That wild bunch is busted up,' grunted Haggerty. He held one arm loosely by his side where a bullet had cut into the flesh, but his eyes were still bright and there was a Colt in the other hand with a wisp of smoke still trailing from it. 'We've got nothin' to fear from these outlaws any more. I reckon the town will wake up tomorrow morning and find itself clean for the first time in a great many years.'

Rick laid the girl gently on the tongue of one of the wagons. She had regained consciousness, looked about her for a moment, not sure where she was, then swung her gaze swiftly to Rick. 'What happened? I remember standing at the top of the stairs and then something hit me. I—'

'You're all right now, Julie,' he said softly. 'Everything is going to be fine.'

He saw the faint smile come to her lips, saw her face lift a little. In her eyes, he read the answer to a lot of questions that had been in his mind ever since he had seen her that night her father had been shot by one of Lenniger's men. A lot had happened since then, he reminded himself. He had ridden away from Hammer Bend and had not expected ever to return to the town; yet fate had decreed otherwise, had brought him back, and now he knew that he did not want to leave. It was going to be a good town in which to live. The lawless element there had been broken for good and he did not think the townsfolk would ever let them gain the upper hand again.

He felt the pressure of the girl's hands on his. There was silence in the street now and already, some of the men were going forward, to where the dead lay in the shadows.